THE LAST DANCE
AND OTHER STORIES

THE LAST DANCE
AND OTHER STORIES

Victoria Hislop

First published 2012 by Headline Review
This Large Print edition published 2013
by AudioGO Ltd by arrangement with
Headline Publishing Group

Hardcover ISBN: 978 1 4713 4948 5
Softcover ISBN: 978 1 4713 4949 2

British Library Cataloguing in Publication Data available

Printed and bound in Great Britain by
TJ International Ltd

For Vasso Sotiriou

With special thanks to:

Elena in Agios Nikolaos, Crete
Ian, Emily and William Hislop
Evripidis Konstantinidis
David Miller
Costas and Alexandra Papadopoulos
Flora Rees
Zoie Sgourou
Thomas Vogiatzis

Author's Note

Some of these stories touch on the current economic crisis in Greece, which is causing extreme hardship to ordinary people. Readers might like to read about the work of the following charitable organisations:

The Smile of the Child: www.hamogelo.gr

Caritas, a Catholic charity currently working in the southern suburbs of Athens: www.caritas.org

The Salvation Army, which is now operating in Athens and Thessaloniki: www.salvationarmy.gr

Contents

The Priest and the Parrot

Stavros had chosen to be celibate. He knew plenty of priests who were married and had children, even some who had fathered children without a wife, but there was already a woman in his life, in whose name he served: the Panagia, the Virgin Mary, the Mother of God.

A year earlier he had arrived in Ladrisi to assist Papa Apostolos, the octogenarian who had been the village's spiritual shepherd for more than fifty years. When he died he was greatly mourned, but Stavros more than adequately took over his duties.

In his care was a parish comprising a village of no more than four hundred, and three nearby hamlets, each of them with its own minuscule church. The priest's house was set up on a hill, on the edge of the village, two minutes' walk from the church, and from this vantage point he could see the other smaller churches that were part of his remit, scattered in the valley below. The young man, who was fresh from the seminary, thanked God for blessing him with such a tranquil parish.

Plenty of women made their way out of the village and up the path to his home. They kept him supplied with dishes of warm food and jars of sweet preserves and would happily have brought him their company too, but he shied away from any contact that might be misconstrued as friendship.

In most rural places, women seemed to outnumber men by at least two to one. There were women on doorsteps, women in the market places, even women toiling in the fields or gathering wood in the forests. In the village where Stavros lived, there seemed even fewer men than was the norm.

Except for funerals and memorial services, he only glimpsed men as he passed the *kafenion*. He would nod, sometimes pass the time of day, but never stop.

On the hill behind his house Papa Stavros had his own beehives which he expertly tended, a skill he had learned from his grandmother, and he always carried a small jar of dark, almost treacle-black honey when he went to visit the sick. He would mix for them a hot, sweet, comforting potion, to which he would add herbs and a squeeze of lemon juice using fruit from his own tree. By the end of his first year as priest, the widows of the village gave their verdict: this young man had remarkable powers.

They trusted in the inspiration behind his teaching, and were transported by the purity of his chanting, but the efficacy of his simple 'medicine' was what really gave them faith. His reputation for healing spread among the women, and the church was constantly illuminated by hundreds of candles. These days the big wooden box with the narrow slot for coins had to be emptied each week, and supplies of the dark, ochre candles needed constant replenishment. They regarded Papa Stavros as a miracle-worker.

When they were sick, the men of the village took a different kind of medicine. They cured their aches and pains with raki, a fire water that seemed to banish all germs, and scorned the women's faith in the priest's remedy. It was, after all, just honey and water, they said.

'Holy potion, crazy notion,' they laughed.

'Still, it does no harm,' said one.

'Whatever keeps them happy,' agreed another.

Papa Stavros had a thicket of a beard that

completely obscured the lower half of his face, and beneath his tall black hat a flowing mass of black curly hair that ended just above his shoulders. Through this densely hirsute landscape, the priest's eyes shone as black as ripe olives. There were a few creases around them which were the inevitable result of having to squint against the sunshine, but his hands revealed his youth. They were as unlined as the skin of a newborn.

In the evening, when his visits were completed and he had performed all his priestly duties in his four churches, he returned home to eat. This was when he most benefited from the love and adoration of the local women. Almost every day, something was waiting for him: a small pot with some bean stew, *fasolakia*, some soup or even a *kleftiko*, a ready-to-eat combination of meat and vegetables. They would come to collect the dish the next morning, so he was in the habit of leaving it outside, washed and ready for collection. And after he had eaten, he would spend the rest of the evening reading the Septuagint, the bare bulb in the ceiling providing only just enough light, even for his young eyesight.

*   *   *

One day in May, an epidemic broke out that Papa Stavros could do nothing to curb. The village school, a single room where twenty-five children were huddled close to learn their lessons, was the perfect environment for the spreading of such a sickness. Kyria Manakis, the new teacher, noticed that three siblings had come out in a rash and gently suggested that they should stay home the following day. Her youth and inexperience meant that she had not acted quite fast enough. Their mother should have been called immediately, but those few extra hours in the classroom allowed the virus free rein. Within a day, measles had swept through the village school like an outbreak of plague and the classroom was half empty. Katerina Manakis was obliged to close the school but diligently gave each child who was still well some exercises to do at home and a book to read.

Gradually the children recovered—but just as they were due to return for the end of the summer term, the teacher herself noticed a tell-tale rash on her chest. She languished for a week alone in her home, with feverish temperatures and spots that covered her entire body. The widow who lived next door called a doctor from a nearby town. He got out his stethoscope, peered into her throat, felt her glands and then crossed the room to wash his hands in her sink. If she did not turn a corner within a few days, she would need to go to hospital, he said.

On the tenth day of her sickness, when the doctor had administered more antibiotics than even he considered safe, Papa Stavros visited.

Katerina Manakis was aware of a bright shaft of light falling across her bed as her front door was opened and sunshine flooded into the darkness. In the semi-delirium of her sickness, she mistook the flash of light for a divine apparition.

'Katerina,' whispered the old widow who lived next door and was keeping an eye on the teacher. 'The priest has come.'

With the widow's help and an extra pillow, Katerina sat up in bed. The light in the room was filtered through the curtains but across the room she saw the priest warm some water, pour it into a glass, stir in a little honey and finally sprinkle in a few herbs.

He spoke very gently to her and took her limp and sweaty hand. She felt the marble-cool fingers and when she drank the tincture that he offered her, it was as though her fever fell away. Papa Stavros visited each day for a week. He was a man of few audible words but prayed silently as he sat at her bedside, his head bowed. With each day her temperature dropped and her rash receded and within a fortnight she was on her feet, owing her recovery to God and to the miracle-working priest.

*   *   *

Katerina Manakis was sad when she realised that she would no longer hear Papa Stavros' businesslike tap on her door, but was glad to be convalescing and to feel her strength growing in the constant warmth of the summer days. She found herself surveying the street in case the priest appeared and guiltily hoped that one of the widows in the street would soon be in need of his healing powers.

As soon as she was strong enough, Katerina Manakis went to the nearest town to buy a small, beaten silver image of a woman to put beside the icon of the Virgin. She would hang it on a narrow ribbon next to dozens of other silver *tamata* in the church which had been left as supplications or thanks for answered prayers. There were images of hearts and hands, feet, arms, legs; in fact every part of the body. There were also many dozens of small silver babies. Over the years, every woman in the village had prayed for successful conception or thanked the Panagia for a beautiful infant who now kicked his legs in a wooden crib.

For the first time since she had come to the village, Katerina found herself sitting on a doorstep with the elderly ladies. She would notice them flush slightly whenever the priest approached, observing how they looked down a little bashfully at the cobbled street when he stopped to greet them. To her mild shame, Katerina realised that she was doing the same.

'He's so handsome,' said one.

'Yes, he's a very fine young man,' sighed another.

'Such wonderful eyes,' said a third. 'Like melting chocoate.'

As widows, they never felt it was wrong to lust after the priest.

Katerina kept her thoughts to herself, fondly remembering his quiet voice and his silent prayers. She watched his retreating figure and reflected that he looked like a man who was happy with his own company.

In spite of his solitude, Stavros was not as lonely as other priests in the same situation. The reality was that he did not live alone. He had a constant companion: a parrot. Nikos was already in residence when the young priest had arrived. Some of the villagers said that the parrot had been in the old priest's family even before Apostolos' birth. So there was speculation that the bird might be well over one hundred years old.

The magnificent blue-green parrot was a fierce creature and mildly cantankerous. He guarded the house more aggressively than a mastiff. When a widow crept up to the door with Stavros' dinner, she would hear a terrifying squawk from within, warning her that she had come far enough. That was why they always left their offerings on the doorstep.

Cats hung about outside, sometimes attracted by the smell of meat. Occasionally, one of them would jump onto the ledge and see the bird inside, staring at them with a beady eye, but when they heard him screech they would slink away.

The parrot had a range of phrases. His own name ('*Ni*ko, *Ni*ko'), the name of his original owner and now 'Stavros'. Occasionally he would also say '*Panagia mou*', which could be an expression of piety but also a gentle expletive, depending on how it was said. With the parrot it was hard to tell. It did not sound pious.

Nikos, whose wings had been clipped many years before, remained all day on his perch, which stood in the centre of the single-room dwelling. During the evening, when the priest was there, he would come down from the perch and flap in an ungainly fashion from the back of one chair to another. He was even given a place at the table with his own enamel plate, on which Stavros placed half a slice of bread. When he was not pecking, he would gaze at his owner, head tilted slightly to one side, with a look that was somewhere between devotion and disdain.

Usually the priest would read while he was eating, but in the past few weeks he had been distracted. He carried his plate to the sink, the food half eaten.

'I can't stop thinking about her, Niko,' he said, running the plate under cold water. He might as well have been talking to himself, but he was comforted that there was some kind of response from the bird.

'*Ni*ko! *Ni*ko! Ti *kan*eis; *Ni*ko!'

The parrot tipped his head on one side, his eyes flickering. He flapped his wings, edged off the table and hopped onto the back of one of the chairs, turning his back on Stavros. He liked to be on his perch by dark and it was now ten o'clock.

Before going to bed himself, Stavros washed his face and hands in the kitchen sink; if he wanted hot water, he had to boil it on the small gas stove. He then lay down to sleep on the couch, which was built into the wall on the other side of the room.

He had never suffered from insomnia in his life. Each day was full, with visits, reading and prayer, so he went to bed tired out, but lately he had found himself tossing and turning, unable to relax. In the early hours, when he finally succumbed, he was pursued by visions of the young teacher and constantly muttered in his sleep.

Usually sunrise or the chiming of the church bell, whichever happened first, would wake him. Nowadays he woke himself calling out her name. Such disturbed slumber gave him little refreshment and in the morning he was almost too exhausted to leave the house. This continued for many weeks.

Nikos' nights were as fitful as the priest's. For a while he would doze, but he was roused every time his master cried out, flapped his wings anxiously, pecked at the seeds in his bowl and shifted from foot to foot.

The weeks passed and Katerina Manakis was growing stronger. The summer days were starting to cool and in a few days it would be time for the school to open once again and she would be there at the front of the class, fully restored, smiling, her dark, braided hair gleaming. The day before school was due to begin, she walked up to the priest's house to leave a portion of chicken with mountain greens that she had made. As she approached, the pack of skinny cats darted guiltily away.

Then, quite audibly, she heard her name being called: 'Kate*ri*na! Kate*ri*na!'

The priest never locked his door, so she turned the handle, pushed it open and went in. There did not seem to be anyone there, but in the half-darkness she could see the glint of an eye.

'*Ni*ko! Kate*ri*na! *Ni*ko! Ti *kan*eis? Ti *kan*eis?'

The young woman's heart felt as if it would burst from her chest. Then she laughed out loud.

She had heard that the young priest had a parrot. Other people had mentioned it to her. But she had never pictured such a large and exotic creature. And she realised that it was the bird who had spoken her name. She smiled, mystified.

As she turned to leave, she heard her name again. This time the voice came from behind her.

'Kyria Katerina. *Kalimera*.' It was the priest. 'I'm so glad to see you're strong enough to take a stroll.'

Katerina was mortified. She was standing in the middle of the priest's house, like a burglar caught red-handed.

'Yes, I am much better.' she said, flustered. 'Look . . . I just brought you something, as a thank you. That's why I'm here.'

'That's very kind. I'm so well nourished in this village,' he said, taking the pot from her. 'I've never eaten like this in my life.'

It felt strange to be talking to a woman right in the heart of his home, a woman who shyly held out a dish of warm food to him, whose eyes sparkled and whose cheeks were flushed.

'But the only reason I came in was . . . I heard someone calling me, so I opened the door, and . . .'

'What do you mean?'

'I heard my name . . . At least, I thought I did.' Katerina flushed. She felt very ashamed, embarrassed even. What on earth would the priest think of her?

Nikos was slow to learn, but once something stuck in his vocabulary, he could never unlearn it.

'Ti *kan*eis? Kate*ri*na! Kate*ri*na! *Ni*ko!'

Stavros looked at the parrot and then at Katerina. How could he explain this? Except for his own name, the bird had not learned a single new word since he had arrived. Until now.

The priest and the parrot held each other's gaze.

'Niko!' said the priest, laughing. 'I didn't know you had learned a new word.'

'Ti *kan*eis? Ti *kan*eis?'

'Very well, thank you,' he replied, smiling broadly. He wanted to add: 'Better than I've ever felt before.'

When he turned round, he realised that Katerina had already slipped out of the house. He could see that she was already halfway down the street and began to hurry after her. There had been no 'goodbye'. Words had been left hanging.

Then he stopped. There was no need to rush.

'I'll return her dish tomorrow,' he said to the bird.

Nikos tilted his head and puffed out his bright turquoise feathers.

The *Kafenion*

The *kafenion* in Kournia had opened for the first time in 1935. Old Kyriakos Malkis had quite simply turned the front room of his house over to the business and moved his family upstairs. Small tables and wooden chairs were arranged on the ground floor and a few more were added to fill the space on the pavement outside. The local carpenter built the bar and there was a long discussion over whether he should also create a sign to put up outside. In the end, it was agreed that the presence of people sitting at tables and chairs made it self-evident: this was 'The *Kafenion*.'

In the winter customers would sit indoors, enjoying the warmth of a wood-burning stove, and in the searing heat of summer they would retreat indoors to catch a modicum of breeze from a slowly turning ceiling fan. There was a young plane tree, a *platanos*, outside and in time it grew and gave them some shade.

Gradually, the strength of old Kyriakos' raki and the excellence of his coffee attracted business even from outlying hamlets. He invested in half a dozen sets of *tavli* and men came for hours at a time to drink, smoke and play.

Quite often, the only 'voices' were those of counters tapping on wood.

Kyria Malkis and the daughter, Maria, kept to the back room, a dingy space concealed behind a piece of ever-darkening lace, and continually washed glasses, cups, saucers and ashtrays in a stone sink, using water carried up the street from the pump in the village square.

When the old folk died, the *kafenion* became

Maria's. Through good planning and a little foresight on the part of her father she was already engaged to one of the customers, Stephanos Papadenos. The promise of the business had made an excellent dowry, and the young man was happy to find himself behind the bar rather than in front of it and quickly adapted to his role as *kafetzis*. It was a simple but perfect life for them both, living, working and socialising in the same few square metres.

Maria and Stephanos continued to run the *kafenion* in the same way as her parents had done. The only alteration they made was to exchange the screen of old lace for a curtain of multicoloured plastic ribbons, which made it much easier to come and go into the back room. They were pleased with the effect, which added a splash of life to the generally brown and beige colour scheme.

As tourism boomed on the island during the 1970s and 1980s, so did the *kafenion*.

Kournia occupied a spectacular position, high up on a hill, with a view across a fertile plain down towards the sea, and in summer tourists would happily travel forty kilometres from the main town of the island for a glimpse of authentic Cretan life and perhaps to buy a tablecloth, its edge expertly crocheted by one of the local women. A couple of other cafés opened in the village but 'The *Kafenion*' occupied the best position. The plane tree had grown and customers enjoyed its deep shade.

In the mid-1980s, when she was well into her forties, Maria gave birth to twin boys. She never revealed to Manos and Petros which of them had been born first and the truth was that she was not actually sure herself. The babies were laid side by side in a small cot in the hospital and after they had been picked up and put down a few times, neither nurses nor parents had the slightest clue which one was which.

They were a great blessing to the couple and, in time, they even became an added commercial advantage when, as five year olds, they would appear in their matching outfits to clear the tables. They went to school in a small nearby town, and by the time they were fourteen they could speak a little English, French and German, enough to have short but rather endearing conversations with tourists and even to take their orders. They vied with each other to see who could make the most tips, but at the end of each week their parents scrupulously divided their earnings to give them equal amounts. Even though they protested, they learned to accept.

When the boys finished school, it seemed that the *kafenion* was not busy enough to justify their staying in the village. With great regret, since they both loved their home and had no desire to leave, they went to live with their older cousin in the island's main town. Manos found a job in a computer shop and Petros worked for the cousin, who ran a supermarket. Every summer, they kept the promise they had made to their parents to spend the month of August helping them.

The *kafenion* remained unchanged. The aging proprietors could see no reason for making innovations when customers seemed to like things as they were. For many years, the only alterations ever made were to the price list which was chalked up on a board, and these changes simply reflected inflation. Then in 2002, the euro was introduced, causing great confusion and consternation. It also demanded the purchase of a new, electronic till. While attempting to carry it across the threshold, Stephanos tripped. It was a bad fall and the local doctor prescribed bed-rest for as long as was necessary.

When it became clear that their father would not be on his feet for some time, a call from their mother was enough to bring the boys hurrying home.

'I'm happy to come back and run the *kafenion* for you,' offered Manos.

'So am I,' offered Petros quickly. 'It's just a phone call to the boss—'

'Our shop is laying people off anyway,' interrupted Manos.

'So is ours!' countered Petros.

Maria Papadenos was touched by her sons' eagerness to help. She was torn, however, between her desire for their return and maternal ambition.

'You mustn't give up your careers!' she said. 'Your father will be on his feet soon enough. And I'll manage till then. It's not such a busy time of year.'

She had to reverse this decision a few months later, when it turned out that the doctor had failed to realise the seriousness of her husband's injuries. As well as a broken leg, he had cracked a number of ribs and a persistent cough turned out to be the result of a punctured lung. The latter proved fatal. Maria called the twins as soon as she realised how little time Stephanos had and they raced back to the village at breakneck speed, both arriving at precisely the same moment, in time to say farewell to their father and then to console their grief-stricken mother.

The funeral was held, and for the forty days until the memorial service had taken place the *kafenion* remained closed for the first time in almost seventy years.

Maria knew that her working life was over and withdrew upstairs to mourn in the darkness of a shuttered room. It was time to hand over the business to her sons.

During the first few months of the reopening, Manos and Petros kept the *kafenion* exactly as it had been under their parents and grandparents. Then after a while they began to discuss some suggestions for modernisation. Having now lived in a bigger town, they both had new ideas.

Should there be a wider range of drinks? Should they make iced coffee? Serve Italian coffee as well as Greek? Every discussion they had ended in disagreement and, in her silent space upstairs, the bereaved Maria Papadenos heard the sound of their altercations.

'I think we should give it a lick of paint.'

'It doesn't need it.'

'What about some new furniture then?'

'There's nothing wrong with what we have!' snapped Petros.

'At the very least let's get some of those moulded plastic chairs. These old things are so *dated*,' Manos shouted, pointing at the traditional straw-seated *psathini* chairs all round the *kafenion*. 'And uncomfortable!'

'They don't seem to keep customers away,' grunted Petros. 'But we should get a new coffee machine.'

'What's the point? Everyone likes Greek coffee.'

'Not everyone,' his brother retorted.

Whatever suggestion one came up with, the other would disagree. Maria listened to the arguments rage and could not even distinguish the voice of one twin from another—their voices combined to make a single discordant noise.

These rows went on for many weeks until she was exhausted by them. Even when she pressed her hands against her ears, the intolerable, squabbling sound of the two people she loved most in the world still penetrated.

One day, when she had been driven almost to despair, an idea began to form in her mind. Within a week she had a plan of action.

* * *

In the months since their father's unexpected death, the twins had not returned to their cousin's house to collect their belongings.

'I'm happy to take over for a couple of days,' she said, 'while you go and collect your things.'

'Are you sure?' asked Manos.

'I'll be fine,' she said. 'It'll make a change.'

'We'll be back this time tomorrow,' Petros assured her.

Maria Papadenos watched her sons get in their cars.

'Drive carefully,' she appealed to them. '*Kalo taksidi!* Bon voyage!'

The antipathy had grown so strong between them, she feared that one would drive the other off the road.

As soon as they had sped off round the corner, she went back inside the *kafenion* and picked up the telephone. It was six thirty in the morning, and a little early for any customers to have arrived.

'*Kalimera*, Kyrie Vandis,' she said. 'Yes, they've gone.'

Within a few minutes, a van drew up and two men got out.

'Thank you so much for coming,' she said, in greeting. 'We know what needs to be done, don't we?'

Over the next few hours, the two carpenters (the son of the man who had constructed the original bar back in 1935 and his nephew) made swift progress. Everything had been pre-planned and they worked fast. First of all they built a partition wall that exactly bisected the *kafenion* and passed through the centre of the bar itself, dividing it neatly into two. Then they put in a second door, identical to the existing one. Finally, they knocked a new hole in the back wall and divided the inner kitchen space.

Customers passed by during the day and were disappointed to find that their *kafenion* was closed for business. Maria was there to explain.

'It's the only solution,' she told them. 'My dear Stephanos and I always made sure that everything was equal for them,' she said, crossing herself as she mentioned her late husband. 'Cutting things exactly in half: bars of chocolate, oranges, pieces of cake. It always avoided argument in the past, and it seems I have to do the same now.'

That evening, the carpenters' wives both came to help and, while the men worked through the night to paint the dividing wall, the women began to split the *kafenion*'s inventory. By the time the twins returned, everything would have been equally shared down to the last ouzo bottle, coffee cup and teaspoon.

At six o'clock in the morning, it was done. The boys had said they would be back at seven thirty, in time to open up for the day.

'Don't you need some signs, now that there are two cafés?' asked the older carpenter.

Maria shook her head.

When they returned, Petros at seven fifteen and Manos only minutes later, they could immediately see that something had changed.

'You've put in a new door!' exclaimed Manos.

'One for "In" and the other for "Out"?' joked Petros.

Maria said nothing and watched as he tried the new door. Once he was inside, it was apparent to Petros what she had done.

'I had no choice,' she told them, firmly. 'I have created a *kafenion* for each of you, to make things fair. I know your father would have approved.'

Both twins remained silent, but the astonishment showed on their faces.

'Manos, yours is this one, and Petros, yours is the other,' she added, authoritatively and alphabetically.

At the beginning some of the customers were a little baffled. They were creatures of habit and had been sitting in the *kafenion* in Kournia for almost their whole lives. They soon got used to the change, however, and respected Maria Papadenos' request that they should frequent both. If someone had always sat on a chair by the door, they continued to do so, even if it was next to different doors on different days.

For the first weeks, it seemed as if the plan had worked perfectly. Maria had shared everything precisely, and even the *platanos* spread an equal shade on the chairs and tables outside. Soon they each hired someone to give them a hand.

One day, Petros glanced across at his brother's *kafenion* and noticed something. By the side of Kyrios Vandis' glass there was a little plate covered with slices of juicy *loukanika*, the spicy mountain sausage. Petros watched the juice run down the man's chin as he swallowed the first mouthful before loading several more onto a single cocktail stick and stuffing them into his mouth. He then took a long slug of Mythos beer and smiled as Manos came outside to take away the empty glass.

'Excellent,' he said, simultaneously with a satisfied belch. 'I'll have another.'

'Right away,' responded Manos, nodding a greeting at his brother, who was standing, arms folded, watching.

Not long afterwards, Manos re-emerged with another beer and, next to it, set down another little plate.

Their father had always insisted on giving customers a few plain almonds or olives (gathered from the trees in their smallholding) with a drink. But Manos was clearly taking the idea of a 'meze' to a new level.

'I see,' thought Petros, spotting the strategy. 'Clever devil.'

The plate that had come out with the second beer had cubes of feta paired with peeled *agouri*, the local cucumber, but even from a distance he could see the sparkling crystals of salt with which they had been sprinkled. No wonder Kyrios Vandis looked so settled in. The effect of the saltiness would create a thirst that could only be slaked by beer. He would soon be trapped in a cycle of need and refreshment.

Within days, Petros had adopted the same technique, but his own complimentary offerings to customers quickly became even more lavish. He marinaded red peppers in wine and oil, fried slim sticks of courgette and sprinkled them with oregano, created tiny meatballs and served them with a yogurt dip and even made dainty filo pastry pies from the local soft *misithra* cheese. All of these appeared next to his customers' drinks, a gift from the *kafenion*.

Manos was not to be outdone, and began to match his brother dish for dish. It was not hard to do. He would reach out across the invisible divide between the tables outside and surreptitiously remove any uneaten morsel left by a customer. Then he would analyse it in his own kitchen.

'Ouzo,' he pronounced triumphantly to Magda, the woman who helped him. 'That's what he has added to this.' He was sampling a tiny left-over cheese pie, which had been dipped into a honey sauce, and he could detect a hint of aniseed, which added to its extraordinary flavour. 'No wonder they go back for more. It's delicious. Original.'

'Don't worry, Manos, we'll find something new,' Magda assured him.

So far, Manos had focused on surpassing the meze that his brother was providing with alcoholic drinks. Now Petros began to create sweet things to be served with coffee. This would be a new way of tempting customers in. They began with a generous cube of *loukoumi*, sprinkled lavishly with icing sugar, and served with tiny cups of strong Greek coffee. The soft, mallowy cubes made by

Olga, Petros' assistant, were almost bigger than the cup itself.

The sweet taste would leave a customer wanting more, and with the inevitable second cup would appear a neat triangle of freshly baked baklava, a small dollop of warm melted chocolate sitting on the top.

The competition became intense, to the customers' advantage if not to the bar owners'. In their neighbouring kitchens, Manos and Petros worked through the night to come up with the most savoury meze and the sweetest *gliko*.

Week on week, the number of customers in each *kafenion* balanced exactly.

When summer came, Petros had a new idea. He knew that tourists liked cocktails and thought that if he could attract the young holiday-makers it would give him the edge over his brother.

He spent a week or so, during the few hours when the *kafenion* was closed, mixing up and testing his recipes.

It did not take long for the first tourists to spread the word and increasing numbers came up from the nearby resorts to have a drink. Manos saw them sitting there with their huge glasses full of brightly coloured liquid and began to form his own plan.

'It won't be hard to do,' he said to Magda. 'I just need a few paper umbrellas and some chopped-up fruit and I can do the same.'

Within a few days, he had created his own cocktail menu. Some of Petros' drinks had suggestive names, 'Sex on the Beach' for example, but Manos' were much more blatant. He had seen how some of the girls who came up from the nearby resort giggled and blushed with pleasure as they ordered the drinks. The cocktail menu was in English only and he knew that the older people of the village who only spoke Greek would be spared any offence. They would have no idea what the pornographic names meant.

Petros retaliated by establishing a 'Happy Hour', when all drinks were half price. And so their war went on, and the weeks turned into months.

Business in the two *kafenion*s continued to balance. Both establishments thrived and the turnover at each of them individually was greater than the entire profit for the original had ever been. Maria Papadenos was delighted by this, but continued to be sad that the competition between her equally beloved boys continued to rage. It was like a fire in their hearts. They had not spoken since the day they had returned from town to find the *kafenion* had been divided. She was only grateful that they could now afford to rent a house each at opposite ends of the village.

* * *

When the tourists had gone and the obscene cocktail menu been put away, Manos decided to spruce up his *kafenion*. With the winter approaching, his customers would be spending more time inside.

When Kyriakos Malkis had painted the place, the only available colour was a dull cream which, over the years, had yellowed with nicotine and age. Manos worked through the night and with a giant can of white emulsion and a roller he swiftly covered the stained anaglypta. Soon the place was transformed. He repainted the bar in a bright blue and resolved to paint the frames of two chairs each night until they were all in matching azure.

The effect was dramatic. It was as if he had doubled the size of the space. Within a day, Petros had done the same, but he chose a minty green for the bar and chairs. On the gleaming white walls he hung some attractive abstract pictures.

Some of the older people did not like these innovations, but they soon forgave the changes. The important things for them were the delicious olive pastries or tender pieces of smoked pork that they now expected with their drinks.

When April came, it was a whole year since the twins had spoken. The two-year memorial service was held for their father, and Maria watched her beloved sons stand side by side in silence. If her husband's death had not already broken her heart, the acrimony between her sons would have done so.

May arrived and, with it, warmer nights. It was the perfect month that came and went before the arrival of the tourists.

One evening, the first of the year when everyone was outside, a visitor to the village sat himself down on one of Petros' freshly painted mint-green seats. Soon he was chatting and laughing with some of the regular customers.

Propped up against his seat was a small case.

'You play?' asked one of the customers.

'Yes,' he replied. 'It's my livelihood. That's why I never let her out of my sight.'

The stranger opened the case and removed his lyra, adjusted one of the pegs by a semitone and began to play.

Every customer in the entire place stopped

talking, leaned back in his seat and listened, spellbound by the sound. For nearly thirty minutes the player's bow glided from one melody to another, and when he stopped for a brief pause he saw that two other men had joined him: one with a bouzouki and another with a drum. He smiled and led them immediately into a traditional tune that was known to them all.

People began to clap. Then chairs and tables were pulled back to create a space around the musicians and some of the younger men got up to dance, forming a circle that began to spin, slowly at first and then with increasing speed. The music knew no boundaries.

Manos stood, arms folded, observing the stranger.

When he had arrived, the visitor had been a customer in Petros' *kafenion*, but now Manos was not so sure. He seemed to have drifted into his own.

Petros watched too.

Though entirely immersed in the music, the player surveyed the scene and smiled. He noted the similitude of the two proprietors, who were only distinguishable by the colour of their shirts. Hair and moustache were identically trimmed.

In the breath between two tunes, he raised his glass, first to Petros and then to Manos.

On this balmy evening, the music drifted upwards and the circle of dancers drifted outwards beyond the confines of the *kafenion*s and into the street. Icy beers and carafes of chilled raki flowed through the night and, from an open window upstairs, Maria Papadenos watched.

By morning, when the party was over, and

the lyra player had gone on his way, there was a confusion of chairs. The blue ones seemed to be where the green had been, and green had mingled with blue. Within a week the wall was down.

Aflame in Athens

This story was inspired by the demonstrations in Athens that took place in late 2008.

Irini hurried through the quiet streets of Plaka and the sound of her heels resonated off the smooth marble. The exposed metal tips clacking on the ancient paving slabs grated on her ear but she had no time to visit the cobbler now. Trainers had not been appropriate today and these were her only pair of smart shoes and the only footwear that went with her neat green coat.

In this old part of Athens, racks of dusty postcards had been optimistically set down on the pavement, carried outside each morning by the owners of the shops who seemed unbothered that the summer tourists had now gone home and that they were unlikely to sell more than a handful each day. They were still resolutely hanging out their Parthenon T-shirts, posters with quotes from Aristotle and maps of the islands, and knew their expensive copies of museum artefacts would be dusted but not sold.

Irini enjoyed walking through this city. To her it was still new and she loved to get lost in the narrow streets that would lead her to the centre of Athens and its long, wide avenues.

It was her godmother's saint's day and she was on her way to meet her at one of Athens' smartest cafés, Zonars. 'Don't forget to buy her some flowers,' her mother had nagged down the telephone the previous night. 'And don't be late for her.' Even from hundreds of kilometres away in Kilkis, Irini's parents dictated the minutiae of her life and Irini, always dutiful, had done as instructed and carried an ornately wrapped arrangement of carnations.

The streets were quiet that morning and it was only when she saw several groups of police loitering, chatting, smoking and murmuring into walkie-talkies that she remembered why some of the main streets had been closed to traffic. There was to be a march that day.

The traffic had been diverted away from the centre in good time. It was uncannily peaceful. For once there was no impatient honking of car horns, no whining of scooters to break the silence and you could almost hear the paving stones breathe. The streets were rarely empty like this. Whether it was four in the afternoon or four in the morning, there would be queues of cars revving at the lights, impatient to get home. Only demonstrations could halt the Athens traffic.

By the time Irini reached her destination in Panepistimiou, one of the long avenues that led down to the main square of Syntagma, she could hear a low, distant rumble. She noticed the police stirring into action, stubbing out half-smoked cigarettes with the heel of a boot and picking up riot shields that had been leaning against shop windows. That almost imperceptible sound would soon turn into a roar.

Irini quickened her pace and soon the café was in sight. Pushing against the heavy glass door, she went inside. Oblivious to the ever-increasing noise in the street, well-heeled customers continued to drink their coffee, served by uniformed waiters.

Irini's *nona*, Dimitra, was already seated at one of the tables by the window, elegant in her red suit, heavy gold earrings and freshly coiffed hair. She was delighted to see her goddaughter. 'You look so well! So smart!' she cried. 'How is university? How are your parents? Are your grandparents well?' One question tumbled out after another.

It was only a few weeks since her term had begun and Irini was still forming her impressions, getting accustomed to this new life, away from her sleepy home town in the north and the tight control of a strict father who had dictated the details of her existence. She had not stepped entirely outside the cloister of family life, however.

'Why pay for some tatty flat,' her father had boomed, 'when your grandparents only live half an hour from university?'

For this reason, like many undergraduates, Irini was in an apartment which had been familiar to her for all nineteen years of her life, with pastel-coloured stuffed toys neatly lined up on her pillow and childhood picture books lined up next to her philology textbooks; every object, on every surface, including the small vases of silk flowers, was perched on a circle of lace crocheted by her grandmother.

It already stretched her parents' means to be putting her through university, so she had been obliged to admit this was a good solution. Her father had a government pension which meant that they were not hard up, but any savings had already been spent on giving his children all the private tuition they had needed after school. Like most Greeks, they were fiercely ambitious for their offspring.

It almost hurt to see her brother's graduation photograph in pride of place above her grandparents' electric fire, knowing that they would be so happy when they had another to place next to it. Her grandmother had already bought the matching frame.

'Why do you have so many pictures of us?' she asked one day as they sat at the mahogany dining table.

'For when you aren't here,' answered her grandmother.

'But I'm always here!' she replied.

'Not in the day,' interrupted her grandfather. 'You aren't here in the day.'

In that moment, she felt suffocated, strangled, by the all-encompassing security her family gave her.

'It's great,' she said now to Dimitra. 'I'm really enjoying everything . . . a little strange some of it, but it's good, it's good. I'm getting used to it all. My grandmother's *dolmadakia* are the best in the world.'

Every child was brought up to think that their grandmother's stuffed vine leaves were second to none and Irini was no different. They ordered their coffee *metrio*, slightly sweet, and small pastries, and chatted about lectures and the syllabus.

From their table by the window, Irini had a good view up the street and she noticed that a group of photographers had gathered outside Zonars. As the phalanx of marchers approached, their cameras flashed in the faces of those who led the march. They were hungry for the following day's front-page image.

The noise from the street was muffled by the dense plate glass that separated the customers of the café from the outside world, but there was a growing sense of threat as the close-packed group of perhaps a thousand students moved steadily closer and now passed in front of them.

The procession had swept along with it a

number of large shaggy dogs. These strays and mongrels that roamed the streets, slept in doorways and lived off restaurant scraps were spinning around barking and yelping at the head of the crowd. A few had been adopted and were held in check by a metre of string, and the canine over-excitement lent chaos to the scene.

The waiters in Zonars stopped working to watch them pass. Their neat, retro outfits, and the tidy rows of gleaming tables seemed a world away from the shambolic crowd that walked by on the other side of the plate glass.

Young men largely formed the brigade of marchers and were almost uniformly in leather jackets, with unshaven faces and closely cropped hair. Their low voices chanted but it was impossible to make out what they were saying and the lettering on their banners was equally incomprehensible. On some of them the fabric was ripped, by accident or design it was impossible to tell, but it added to the sense of potential violence.

'Something to do with education reforms,' muttered the waiter in answer to Dimitra's question, as he scattered her change into a metal saucer on the table.

Irini felt slightly uncomfortable sitting here in this bourgeois café. She too was a student, like the people outside, but the divide seemed immense.

Dimitra noticed her expression change and realised that her goddaughter's attention had drifted away.

'What is it?' she said with concern. 'You mustn't worry about these demonstrations. I know they don't happen in Kilkis but they're a day-to-day occurrence here. These students are always taking to the streets, protesting about something or other.'

She gave a dismissive wave with her hand and Irini felt a gulf open up between herself and her elegant godmother. It seemed wrong to belittle whatever it was that the people outside clearly felt strongly about, but she did not want to argue.

It took fifteen minutes for the protesters to pass, by which time their second coffees were finished and it was time to leave.

'It was so lovely to see you—and thank you for my flowers!' said Dimitra. 'Let's meet up again soon. And don't worry about those students. Just keep your distance.'

As she leaned forward to kiss her, Irini breathed in her godmother's expensive scent. It was like being enveloped in a cashmere blanket. The elegant sixty year old hastened across the road and turned to wave.

'*Yassou agapi mou!* Goodbye, my dear,' she called out.

Irini glanced to her right and saw the tail end of the march still making its way slowly towards the government building, the chanting little more than a low humming now. For a moment she was tempted to follow but this was not the right time and instead she turned left up the empty street. Traffic diversions would continue for another ten minutes so she took the chance to walk down the middle of the road, placing her feet carefully along the white lines. Lights still turned from red to green, but for a few moments she was all alone in this wide avenue, completely and unexpectedly free.

* * *

Several times that week, her classes were half empty as students took time off to go out into the streets. It seemed strange to her, in their first term of university, to waste all these lectures, but it was obvious to Irini when she first stepped inside the foyer that the politics on the street were as important to most of the students as anything they might learn inside the faculty building. Thousands of identical red and black propaganda flyers were posted on the wall, their endlessly repeated message almost lost in an hypnotic pattern.

'Why don't you come with us?' some of them asked her.

As far as Irini's father was concerned there was only one political party, only one view of the world, and to take sides against it, even in an argument around the dining table, took more courage than she would ever have. Communists were detested, anarchists despised. This was the view she had no courage to question, so when a huge group of her fellow students went off regularly and cheerfully with their makeshift banners, she could not join them. For them it was a way of life, passing through the graffiti-daubed corridors where even the walls joined in the protest.

There were many days and nights, though, when marches and politics were forgotten and every student, whatever their views, ate, drank, danced and looked for love.

That Friday night, in a bar in the Exarchia district, Irini caught sight of a pair of pale green eyes. The low light accentuated their pallor. She smiled. It was impossible not to. A perfect face such as this made the world a better place.

He smiled back.

'Drink?' he gestured. The volume of noisy conversation in the bar was almost deafening. Irini and her friends joined his group and introductions were made. The boy's name was Fotis.

The evening passed, with bottles gradually forming a glass forest on the table and smoke curling closely around them. Irini was happy to be meeting some people from other faculties, and even happier to feel the strong beam of this beautiful boy's attention on her. On a raised area in the middle of the room, singers and musicians came and went, their prodigious talent hardly acknowledged by the throng of high-spirited young people.

At four the bar was starting to close and Irini stood up to leave. She knew that one or other of her grandparents stayed awake until she returned and this pricked her conscience. Out on the pavement, though, Fotis took her hand and Irini immediately knew she would not be going home that night. She was always urging her grandmother to believe that she was old enough to take care of herself and tonight she hoped that the sweet octogenarian would take those words to heart.

Close by in a crumbling apartment block, built well before the invention of the lift, Fotis, his flatmate Antonis and Irini climbed nine flights of stairs. The walls were covered with a pattern as intricate as lace, but on close inspection Irini saw that the design was made up of a thousand tiny letters. Just as at the university, even the yellowing walls of the landing screamed a political message.

Irini resisted the urge to look over the low banister rail down into the sickening depths of the stairwell and was relieved when Fotis opened the door to their one-bedroom flat where a trail of dirty crockery led from sofa to sink and the air reeked of stale ash. There was nowhere for the fumes to escape.

Like her, these boys were studying at the university. But there the similarity ended. Irini breathed in the scent of grubbiness, the aroma of this reality, this proper student way of life.

Fotis' windowless flat, with its low ceilings and dark paintwork, seemed far less claustrophobic than her bland if airy home. This struck her on the first and on every subsequent occasion when they strolled back to his place after an evening in the bar. It was always with Antonis that they walked home, three abreast with Fotis in the middle and when they got in, the routine was the same. Antonis would switch on the television and settle down in front of it, pulling his duvet out from underneath the sofa which would then become his bed and Fotis would lead Irini into his bedroom.

In the narrow confines of his bed, she was scorched by the blaze of his passion. It was annihilating, wordless, and the muscularity of his slim body amazed her. This was more than she had ever expected from love.

Not once did she see Fotis during daylight hours. They always met up in the same bar which attracted a huge crowd most evenings and then returned to his dark apartment and unyielding bed. Unlike the bedroom in her grandmother's home, where a gap in the curtains let through a chink of light to wake her, there was no window here. It was the coolness of sheets that disturbed her in the morning, not sunshine. The incendiary heat and sweat of the previous night had chilled the bed linen to icy dampness and the clammy solitude made her shiver. Fotis was never there.

The first few times she got up and crept quietly out of the flat, careful not to wake Antonis, but one morning as she opened the bedroom door, she saw him sitting at the small kitchen table. In these weeks of knowing each other, they had scarcely exchanged a word. Irini had sensed the possessiveness of an established friend and detected a whiff of hostility. It had made her unsure of Antonis and now for the first time they were alone together.

'*Yassou* . . .' she said in friendly greeting. 'Hi . . .'

He nodded in acknowledgement and drew deeply on his cigarette.

Though it was still early, he had put on the radio and the tinny sound of a bouzouki tinkled away in the background. There was a pyramid of cigarette butts in the ashtray in front of him and pale ash sprinkled across the table top like dirty icing sugar.

'Have you seen Fotis?' she asked. 'Do you know where he has gone?'

Antonis shook his head.

''Fraid not,' he said. 'Not a clue.'

Slowly and deliberately he took another cigarette from the packet in front of him and, without offering her one, lit up. He inhaled deeply and looked up at her. She had not really looked at Antonis properly before. He had the same beard and almost-smooth head as Fotis, but in other ways they were very different. She took in that Antonis was broader, rounder, and with a nose that seemed disproportionately small for his wide face.

'Right . . . OK,' she said. 'Bye.'

And with that, she headed out into the pale dawn and walked the few kilometres back to her own home, shivering.

Her friends quizzed her about Fotis, but there was nothing she wanted to tell them. All she knew was that the temperature of her infatuation for him rose by the day and the attention he gave her when they were together was new and over-powering. She accepted that a few days might pass without him contacting her, not even with a text message.

After one such gap in their meetings, she collided with him outside the university. He smiled his broad smile and took her arm.

'Irini *mou*, my Irini, where have you been?'

Disarmed by his friendliness, she felt herself melt beneath the warmth of his hand. As they walked to his flat later that night, he stopped to light a cigarette. In the dark side-street the bright flame of his lighter cast sinister dancing shadows across his face. It was ghoulish, macabre but no more than a trick of the light.

*   *   *

The following dawn, she woke as before to find him gone. Once again, she found Antonis keeping vigil at the kitchen table.

'Don't either of you two need any sleep?' she asked Antonis, trying to make light of it. 'Are you insomniacs or something?'

'Nope,' said Antonis. 'You're not even warm.'

'Right. Well, never mind. It's just odd, that's all. Just odd.'

With that, Irini was about to leave but Antonis had something more to say.

‘Look . . . take care. Please take care.’

His tone of genuine concern seemed strange and she had no idea what to make of it.

Classes at university began to become increasingly disrupted. Even when students turned up to seminars, the professors were not always there to teach and if they were, some of them seemed disappointed in those that had made the effort to come.

‘So you’re not on the march?’ one of them asked her. ‘Why?’

Irini had no answer. Explaining why she was *not* doing something seemed much harder than justifying why she was.

‘I had your seminar to attend,’ was all she could think of to say.

The real reason was her fear of her father’s reaction if she decided to go out on a demonstration. His disappointment would be bitter. And her mother would literally make herself ill with worry. Parading down Panepistimiou and being spotted by her godmother holding a banner was something she would never risk.

In the past few weeks, the reason for marching had changed. The police had shot dead a fifteen-year-old boy in the street and the mood was a new and uglier one. There were many more occasions when classes at the university were empty of students and the streets were full of protest. Now the demonstrations became more violent. In the city centre, the stink of tear gas permeated the streets, shops were being set alight and every cash-point machine had become a blackened hole in the wall. Every capitalist institution was a target and even the city’s huge Christmas tree became a flaming symbol of the protesters' anger.

One evening, after a journey home disrupted by road closures and police barricades, Irini got home later than usual. She crossed the polished floor of the hallway and through a scarcely open door, she caught a glimpse of her grandfather reading in his study. She heard him call her name.

'Is that you, Irini? Come in to see me, would you?'

Even though he had been retired for twenty years, her grandfather still had the manner of a government official and spent many hours each day reading at his desk.

'Let me have a look at you,' he said, scrutinising her face with a mixture of love and curiosity. 'Where have you been?'

'Getting back from the university . . .'

'You seem to be out a lot at the moment. More than usual.'

'It takes a while to get home when there are demonstrations.'

'Yes. These demonstrations . . . That's what I really want to talk to you about. We haven't ever really discussed politics but—'

'I'm not involved in them,' interjected Irini.

'I'm sure you're not,' he said. 'But I know what your faculty is like. It has a reputation, you know. For being radical. And your father—'

'Well I'm not a radical,' she said. 'Really I'm not.'

Even from a distance she could feel the eye of her father on her. Irini knew that he would probably already have heard that she often did not return until light.

A newspaper, which had been the catalyst for

this discussion, lay on her grandfather's desk. She could see the headlines:

CITY CENTRE BLAZES

'Look at what's going on!' said her grandfather.

He waved the newspaper that had been lying on his desk in the air.

'These *koukouloforoi*! These hooded kids! They're a disgrace!' His voice had risen. 'They're *anarchists*!'

The kindly old man could quickly lose his gentle air once he was on this subject.

And then something caught her eye.

There were two images on the front page. One of the burning tree and a second of someone falling beneath the baton blows of two riot police. Their anonymity was guaranteed—their faces were concealed behind the perspex globes of their helmets—but their victim's features were caught vividly on camera, contorted by a mixture of pain and rage. If his eyes had not been so distinctive, so clear, so pale, the image would not have grabbed her attention so forcibly.

She took the newspaper from her grandfather. Her hands were shaking and her heart pounded. It was Fotis. It was undoubtedly him. What shocked her was that in his hand he clung on to a flaming torch. This was making the job of the police, who clearly feared that they might go up in flames, much harder. The picture showed that Fotis' knuckles were white with determination. He was not going to let go of his weapon.

'You see!' said her grandfather. 'Look at that hooligan!'

Irini could scarcely speak.

'It's awful, yes . . . awful,' she whispered.

With those words she put the newspaper back on her grandfather's desk.

'I'm just going out for a while,' she said. 'I'll see you later.'

'But your grandmother has made supper—'

Before he had finished the sentence, the door had slammed.

Irini ran down the street, turned left and right and right again. This time her feet were soundless on the paving stones of Plaka. Twenty minutes later, she arrived, her chest tight with exertion, in a familiar down-at-heel Exarchia street. The outer door to the block was ajar. It had been kicked off its latch some while back and no one had bothered to repair it. She ran up the stairs, two at a time and reached the ninth floor, where she fell against the door to Fotis' flat, hammering on it with all her remaining strength.

A second later, Antonis threw it open.

'Where . . .?' she gasped.

'He's not here,' he said, standing aside to let her pass.

In her panic and confusion, Irini only had two possible thoughts. That Fotis was locked up somewhere or in hospital. It took her some time to take in what Antonis was trying to tell her.

'He's gone. He's gone away.'

'What? Where?'

'Look, you need to sit down. And I will tell you.'

She allowed Antonis to lead her by the arm to the kitchen table where she took one of the two rickety chairs.

'What are these?'

'I found all of these in Fotis' room a couple of days ago.'

'But why were they there?'

'He collected them. I have known him a while but . . .'

Spread out before her on the kitchen table was a series of newspaper cuttings.

'Pendelis . . . Areopolis . . . Artemida . . .
Kronos.'

As she read the place names out aloud, she knew immediately what the link was between them.

'Fire,' she said. 'All devastated by fire.'

'But not just that,' said Antonis. 'Arson was suspected with all of them.'

'And you think Fotis may have something to do with . . .?'

'Well, what do you think?' said Antonis. 'And I suppose you saw this picture on the front of *Kathimerini*?' he added.

'Holding the torch? I did.'

'And look at this.'

Antonis led Irini by the arm towards Fotis' room. As soon as he opened the door, an acrid stench of burning almost choked her. In the middle of the room a small pile of clothes and papers had been burnt. The furniture was blackened, and the bed-clothes still dripped from Antonis' frantic attempts to extinguish the flames.

'My God. He could have set this whole block alight!' she gasped.

'If I hadn't come back when I did . . .'

'How could he?' she said, her throat dry with the shock and the still-lingering fumes from the fire.

'I don't think he cared,' answered Antonis. 'That's the nature of arson. He just wouldn't have cared . . .'

Once again she looked at the picture on the front of the newspaper and examined the familiar features. For all those weeks she had only seen their perfection but now she saw them twisted by an all-consuming rage and noticed again the devilish look she had seen in the street that night. And in that moment the flame went out. Even the memory of it chilled her, right to the heart.

The name 'Irini' means 'Peace', and 'Fotis' comes from the Greek word for 'Fire'.

The *Zacharoplasteion*

In a Melbourne suburb, a young man was unpacking. He retrieved two small objects from the bottom of his suitcase, removed several layers of tissue and placed them carefully on his desk. Apart from a key ring of the Parthenon that he had been given by his aunt, they were his sole souvenir from Greece. The figures, a bear and an eagle, were perfect in every detail and he would treasure them.

* * *

On the other side of the world, Sofia watched her daughter floating down the aisle, all in white, radiant, smiling her angelic smile.

Not just today, but each and every day she saw this same vision.

Angeliki worked with her mother in the family *zacharoplasteion*, and whenever Sofia saw her in the aisles of bread trolleys she would wonder: 'How long?' How long would it be until she married?

Her daughter's skin was as smooth and golden as the loaves, and even when she was coating cherries or almonds in chocolate she managed to avoid splashing her immaculate white coat. She was flawless, and her mother did not understand why such a creature, who was sweeter than a pastry, more perfect than her best baklava, seemed to have been left on the shelf, like last year's biscuits.

Angeliki was twenty-nine now. All her school friends were long since married. All Sofia's friends' daughters and even her friends' nieces had made the sacred journey round the altar.

Sofia's sleeves were rolled up as she kneaded the

bread. She threw the huge ball of dough down on the wooden block and folded in the sides again and again and again, pulling and stretching the rubbery mix of flour and yeast.

'We had an invitation today,' she said to her daughter.

'That's nice,' responded Angeliki. 'Who from?'

'Katerina and Mihali. The baptism of their son.'

'Katerina and Mihali?' Angeliki mumbled, continuing her task of wrapping each cherry in an individual foil.

'You know!' said her mother with irritation. 'Maria's second cousin's daughter and her husband. Their third.'

A moment passed before the young woman responded. She heard similar strings of names often and did not have a clue which Maria this one was. It could have been any one of forty.

'Third cousin?' she said, even more vaguely than before.

'Third *child*, Angeliki! *Third child!*'

'That's nice.'

'What do you mean, "that's nice"?'

'It's nice that they sent you an invitation.'

Angeliki knew as well as her mother did that more than five hundred invitations would have gone out. People were in the habit of inviting the most distant relations and acquaintances to marriages and baptisms.

Sofia tutted. In spite of the love she felt for her only child, her frustration with her sometimes bubbled to the surface.

'Katerina is still only twenty-eight. Three children under three!'

'That sounds like hard work,' commented

Angeliki, which was not the response she was meant to give.

'It might be hard work, *agapi mou*, but it's also a great blessing and a great achievement to have produced three children by that age.'

Angeliki, usually so serene, bit into the last cherry on the tray and allowed the juice to run down her chin.

'*Why* is it an achievement? Producing children seems no more difficult than piping a message on a cake, as far as I can see,' she said. 'It's only doing what comes naturally to some people.'

'Well it obviously doesn't come naturally to *everyone*, does it?' her mother retorted tartly.

The girl and her mother frequently had rows along similar lines. Different things might spark them off, but lurking beneath was the same old question. Why was Angeliki not like other girls? Why was *she* not married?

She was certainly more beautiful than almost all the other girls who lived in Larnapoli. In the summer the tourists would come into town from the nearby seaside resort and she knew that Angeliki had often been invited out by foreign boys, who would spot her through the window of the shop and come in to flirt. But she always said no. She said no to everyone. She had spent her life keeping her distance, as far as her mother could see.

Larnapoli was a bustling town where most residents knew each other and many of them were related in some way. Most of Angeliki's school friends had married boys from their class and the 'pairing up' was a process that had happened several years before. It was rare for newcomers to move into town as there was nothing to bring them.

When she had finished wrapping the cherries, Angeliki joined her mother in the bread-making. Sofia slapped the shiny yellow mass onto the board and plunged in a huge knife to bisect it.

Flour billowed up in clouds as they both dipped their hands in a sack of the pale yellow powder to stop the dough sticking to them. Sofia then threw her whole body weight into the job. She was a powerful woman, not very tall, but probably twice Angeliki's width. Her daughter was more like her late father, who had been slight in build. All Sofia's frustrations were taken out on the dough, which was probably why the bread from Papalenou's was the most popular in town. Good loaves needed almost manly strength, to pump in the air.

Angeliki did not have it in her to treat the dough the way her mother did, and Sofia knew that when the loaves emerged from the oven she would be able to see the difference. Angeliki's loaves lacked conviction and this annoyed her mother on a daily basis.

'Look, why don't you go over there and finish the cake orders,' she snapped. 'Kyria Kalobaki will be coming in soon to collect hers, so you should start with that one.'

No one could fault Angeliki's piping skills. Her sugar-and-water handwriting was fine and elegant. She could have written whole chapters of a book on the top of a cake, and every word would be legible. She was prodigiously dexterous at everything that required a light touch.

Sofia Papalenou felt the changing seasons through her confectionery: in spring, there were the special Lenten biscuits and Easter breads to be baked; then came the summer wedding season and the demand for cakes and the deep fried pastry dipped in honey, *kserotigano*, that was handed out at nuptials. August was also the month when they made their own ice-creams in amazing flavours. Then came autumn which was specially busy for celebratory gâteaux for saints' days, with Stavros, Elpida and Thomas being particularly popular names in this town. After that there were the St Nicholas specialities at the beginning of December, the frantic Christmas period and finally the Vasilopita cakes for the New Year that reminded her that yet another twelve months had gone by and her daughter was still unattached.

Although every order Sofia took helped to fill her till, it emptied her of a little more hope. There might have been plenty of sweetness in her life, but there was a considerable amount of bitterness too.

* * *

Angeliki knew that her single state upset her mother to the point of obsession but, unlike her school friends, the young woman would wait for ever rather than compromise. If her mother could only understand that she applied her perfectionism to every part of life, not just her work, it would help.

Something had happened the previous year that her mother would never understand. It was a moment when everything changed.

A stranger had come into the shop. He was in his mid twenties and, if she had been out front, her mother would have noted a scruffy 'youth' and helped him to whatever he wanted without a second glance. For Angeliki he was unlike any other customer she had ever served.

The majority of Larnapoli's population seemed to exist in a state of misery. At least this was how it seemed to Angeliki, who had watched their dour faces come and go for almost her entire life. Many of them came in silently each day and, in a wordless transaction, were handed their usual order in exchange for coins.

She knew that her mother had long since given up expecting applause for the lightness of her sponges, or the density of her chocolate torte. People came in for their fix of sweetness without appreciating how much went into even the simplest petits fours, and Angeliki often lamented that hours of careful handiwork would be devoured in seconds.

Angeliki remembered the day so vividly. Not many minutes before the stranger arrived, she had come from the kitchen with fresh bread, and started to fill the shelves with loaves. This meant that her back was turned to the shop when the door opened, but she could see him clearly in the mirrored wall. He strolled around, peering into the shiny glass cabinets and studying appreciatively the variety of sweetness on display.

He was not tall (about the same size as her, in fact, maybe one metre seventy), average in build (though more stocky than slim), and with dark silky hair that touched his collar. He had a slight beard, which looked like the result of not shaving rather than a conscious decision, and wore a faded T-shirt and jeans. In her entire life she had not seen a face in which such kindness and beauty were combined. It was almost shocking.

'Can I help you?' she asked politely, trying not to stare at him but aware that her mouth had dried.

'I'd like some of these little cakes, please,' he said. 'What's inside them?'

As she described in detail the various types of flavours and fruits in the miniature tarts, he nodded appreciatively.

'Just one of each, I think,' he said. 'That'll make a dozen, won't it?'

'Ten,' she said. 'There are ten different ones.'

Her hands shook visibly as she folded a box into shape.

He watched her.

'Can I help?'

Though she had made up these boxes a thousand times, this time she seemed to have forgotten how. Suddenly it seemed more complex than origami.

'No, really. It's fine. Honestly.'

She felt embarrassed but looked up and found herself staring straight into his eyes. They were liquorice black.

'I used to work in a bakery once. My grandfather's. I could never make those boxes work,' he said, laughing. 'And I was even more useless when it came to the ribbon.'

She felt herself relax.

'Irresistible,' he said, laughing.

There was a moment's pause as she realised that he was flirting with her.

'And where was your family's *zacharoplasteion*?' she asked, smiling.

'In Kalamata,' he replied. 'Sadly it was sold a while back. But it wasn't a patch on this one.'

One of the tarts landed upside down in the box.

'Oh, I'm so sorry,' she said, her shaking hands making her uncharacteristically clumsy. 'I'll start again.'

'No, no—it's all right. They'll taste just the same. It really doesn't matter.'

He watched her as she worked.

After she had packaged up the little tarts, he then pointed out some biscuits he wanted and then a dozen of the chocolate-coated cherries. He quizzed her on the ingredients in everything and she could feel that his interest was genuine.

'And can I have one of those bears too?' he asked.

'A marzipan one?'

'Yes. They remind me of the ones my grandmother used to make. Can I eat it now?'

She took one from the cabinet, placed it on a napkin and handed it to him. He examined it carefully.

'It's incredible!' he exclaimed. 'My grandmother's were never quite like this. You have even textured the fur!'

Onto every animal, Angeliki had deftly added tiny features. Cats had whiskers, for example, and birds had feathers.

'It doesn't really take that much effort,' she said bashfully.

'But it's fantastic. Too perfect to eat. I'm going to keep it on my desk.'

Angeliki laughed, and he laughed too.

'Let me put him in a box then,' she said.

As she did so, she slipped another creature in beside it. 'He'll need company,' she said.

Eventually, four boxes sat on the counter, tightly fastened with curly ribbon.

'Thank you so much,' he said. 'What do I owe you for all these works of art?'

'Ten euros fifty,' she said, saying the first figure

that came into her head. 'The animals are a gift.'

'That's so kind. I promise to take good care of them.'

'You're meant to eat them!'

'Never. I will eat everything else, but not these. It would be an insult. They might be small, but they're sculptures. Masterpieces!'

His laughter and his good nature completely overthrew Angeliki. For five years she had worked there each day, and not once had she served a customer who made her smile like this. She felt that all the ice-cream in the nearby cabinet would melt in his warmth. As well as taking a delighted interest in what was in the shop, he smiled: a deep, life-loving smile. She had never met anyone who was so relaxed and at ease with himself.

Angeliki slowly counted the change into his hand, aware that she was trying to delay his leaving.

There was a moment—as the final twenty-cent piece fell into his palm—when she looked up and found him gazing at her. She returned his look. Perhaps it was only for a second or two, but it made her feel full, though not in the way she had done as a child when she had eaten too much of her mother's pastries. This was a feeling of completeness.

It was clear that he did not want to hurry away, and she was sure that he hesitated a moment before pulling the door towards him.

'Goodbye,' he said. 'Thank you so much for these.'

The glass panel closed behind him, and he seemed to pause as if he had forgotten something. Then he turned around, lifted his hand to wave and was gone.

Every part of her wanted to run after him, but

there was a yawning gulf between instinct and reason.

That was it. The image of his face had stayed with her, every feature, every detail. For Angeliki it was as if only moments had passed since he had paused on the threshold of the shop and then vanished from sight. Not a day had gone by when she had not thought of him. The memory of his smile was unfading.

He was just a customer passing through, probably visiting a friend or relative in a nearby village and stopping to get them a gift, but she was both made and unmade by the encounter. Nobody else before or since had stirred her in the way he had done.

Some people wondered if she had been hurt by someone and that this was the reason she rejected advances. But Angeliki knew that her heart had been woken, not broken.

The *Periptero*

It was the silent hour. The wind had dropped, traffic had disappeared, pedestrians had vanished. It was hard to tell whether the stray, still dogs in the shade were alive or dead. Flies seemed to be the only living creatures, ceaselessly flitting from one animal to the other.

Shops hid behind metal shutters and all of these were defaced with graffiti. There was an occasional expression of love hidden in amongst all the outpourings of anger against politicians and the world. At this time of day, the street resembled a gallery of abstract art, but one without visitors. Only one 'work' had a clear meaning: *Hunger hurts*.

Panopoli was a typical city in northern Greece. In summer, there was a total absence of tourists, but a relentless presence of sun. An avenue of trees on either side of the street protected pedestrians from the heat, but in the afternoons most of them stayed at home in any case, resting quietly in the darkness of their apartments, before dragging their feet back for a second shift of work in the cool of the day. Everything was shut at this time, apart from the *kafenion* in the central square and the *periptero* at the end of the street.

This kiosk, run by Giorgos Kazaras, had been open for eighteen hours a day ever since he was granted the licence for it in the late 1950s. In those days, it had comprised merely the airless wooden hut with its small 'window' facing the pavement through which people paid and it sold only cigarettes and sweets. Gradually over the next half century he had extended his empire in both directions. The first radical innovation had been a fridge for cold drinks and after that came a freezer for ice-creams. Then followed the baskets full of plastic toys, long-lasting croissants, bags of crisps and packets of biscuits. On the counter he also kept other essentials of life such as toothpaste, chewing gum and condoms, the last in easy reach for the customer so that they did not have to make a point of asking for them.

In addition, there had been an ever-expanding system of racks with newspapers and magazines. The people of this quiet backwater town were hungry for the glamour supplied by Athenian publishers and their brightly coloured publications flew off Giorgos' shelves, selling out within hours of arriving.

In darkened rooms on these listless afternoons, women idly browsed the glossy pages, and daydreamed of encountering celebrities. Giorgos' twenty-one-year-old daughter, Andriani, was a particularly avid consumer of this glamour porn. With her never-ending supply (her father allowed her to read every title as long as she kept the pages pristine, so that he could put them back on the rack to sell), she had been flicking through the shiny pages of these publications before she could even read.

Right up until she died when Andriani was fifteen, Litsa Kazaras, a part-time nurse, fought a losing battle to make her daughter read books, rather than flick idly through magazines. 'They scramble the brain, those silly comics,' she complained to her husband. 'Fine for you to make money from them, but I won't have Andriani's mind ruined.'

Since her mother had passed away, Andriani had

not picked up even a single paperback. Just looking at the images of the glorious blondes and their tanned boyfriends gave her the fleeting illusion that her own life had become more colourful. Naturally she dreamed of being more beautiful, rich and famous and of living somewhere other than Panopoli, but the pictures also made her aspire to more realisable, material goals.

A furniture shop had recently opened on the edge of town, opposite the petrol station. Andriani often strolled over there while the attendant was filling her small car and pressed her nose up against the window, leaving her breath marks behind. It was a huge showroom, stocking expensive and flashy sofas, tables and chairs as well as a selection of lighting, mostly crystal chandeliers. Everything was imported from Italy and was glittering and desirable, and the ranges had names inspired by Hollywood: the 'Beverly Hills', the 'Bel-Air', the 'Mulholland Drive'. Every item looked freshly lifted from the pages of *Hello!*.

Having grown up in an apartment where all the furniture had been purchased in the 1950s and never replaced, Andriani had never sat on anything other than nylon upholstery, most of it hidden beneath crocheted throws and lacy antimacassars. In her imagination, the red leather Chesterfield three-piece suite that filled the window of *Spiti Sou*, Your House, would change her life.

She described it in detail to her father.

'Ba*ba*,' she whined, 'why don't we get one like that? Instead of all that old-fashioned stuff we have?'

'You can have what you want if we find a rich man for you to marry,' he snapped. 'But for now, we have to live with what we have. There's nothing wrong with it. It was good enough for your mother. And that's all there is to it.'

Andriani's window-shopping had not gone unnoticed by the owner, Takis Stakakis. Every time anyone looked into the window, he would study them, unseen in the shadows behind his desk. He reckoned he could calculate the chance of someone's coming through the door just from the kind of car they drove, and if they did come in, he weighed up the likelihood of their spending some money on the basis of their perfume or aftershave. Anything by Gucci and he knew he would be banking a cheque that night. By definition his customers had to be people with both cash and ostentatious taste, rather like himself.

* * *

Andriani had a pretty enough face, with big brown eyes and luxuriant long dark hair that she took an hour each morning to tong into gleaming curls. Although she spent over an hour in front of the mirror before leaving for her part-time job in the local bank, she had not noticed that her clothes were getting a little on the tight side. Along with her generous lips, painted as red as the furniture she so coveted, Andriani's look was one that attracted men like Takis. From his vantage point in the shop, he could see her clearly. Her Lycra top and trousers fitted tightly to her body, in rather the same way that leather was stretched over the padding on his upholstered chairs. Every generous curve was on display.

One day he appeared at the door and invited

her into the shop. The reflective gleam on the plate glass had ensured that he had been hidden in the shadows and his unexpected appearance took her by surprise.

'Please,' he said. 'It's free to come in and have a look. And there's no charge for trying.'

She stood uncertainly for a moment, blushing, as Stakakis continued with his sales spiel.

'It only costs when you want to take something home. And for women with beautiful eyes, there's usually a discount.'

Andriani giggled. Where was the harm?

Soon she was perched on the red leather settee. She crossed her legs, feigning the sophisticated pose that she had seen people adopt in glossy magazines.

'Oh, it's lovely,' she cooed.

'You look very at home,' he said, flattering her. 'Try some others. Why not?'

He could see from the battered little car that was still parked across the street at the petrol station that this girl would never be a customer, but no one else had come in that day and he needed to keep his sales patter well oiled. He knew that women were the ones who made the decisions in the home and that most men had no views about whether a sofa needed replacing or whether they should have six chairs or eight to go round a table. Furniture sales and flirtation went hand in hand.

She had been trying to avoid eye contact, but now that he was sitting down opposite her on a matching armchair, she looked at him through her thick lashes.

Stakakis was slim and wore a well-cut suit, dapper patent shoes which were designed to make his feet look longer and slimmer than they were, and a pale blue shirt undone to the fourth button. She could see the glint of a heavy gold chain round his neck. He was definitely what Andriani would later describe to her colleagues at the bank as 'sexy'. She had failed to notice that the greying wisps on his bronzed chest did not match the jet black hair on his head.

Half an hour passed before she realised that she had to go, but it was enough time for him to have invited her for a drink. She flushed again, almost the colour of the furniture, as she reached out and took his business card.

Later that week, Stakakis collected her in his Porsche Cayenne to take her for the promised drink and the following weekend he whisked her away to a club in a neighbouring town. He did the same on subsequent weekends. Andriani was having the time of her life. It was what she had always dreamed of: a man who took her to places with white leather upholstery, who was directed straight to VIP areas and never failed to pay for her *mojitos*. She soon got used to being abandoned for half an hour at a time. While Stakakis had a quick 'business meeting' Andriani happily killed the minutes repairing her make-up.

Her father disapproved deeply of these outings. It was a small town and people gossiped. Takis Stakakis was an outsider. He had not been born in Panopoli and he did not live there now. The fact that no one knew a thing about him made him an object of suspicion. As far as anyone could recall, he had never stepped over the threshold of a single shop in town. And they would definitely remember if he had ever been inside the *kafenion*. He had been four or five times to the *periptero* but was always in a hurry, parking his huge black car right next to the kiosk and leaving its engine running while he hopped out to buy what he needed, usually a packet of Rothmans Royale and some mints. Within seconds, he had roared off again. The only things that Giorgos had ever noticed about him were an expensive watch protruding from a crisp cuff and a waft of heavy aftershave.

Giorgos could tell that his daughter was infatuated. Even though he did not see very much of her, as he was inside his kiosk all day and most of the evening, when she called by after work, on her way home to make his dinner, she was always smiling. He could not remember her ever being like this, even before her mother had died.

'He's very nice, Baba,' she said, sensing her father's disapproval and eager to win him round. 'And he takes me to these smart places.'

'Where are those then?' Giorgos replied, glancing up from his newspaper.

'All over. Varakis. Even Larissa.'

'Larissa? That seems a bit of a distance for an evening out.'

'Nowhere takes long in his Cayenne,' she boasted, with obvious pride in knowing someone with such a vehicle.

Giorgos grunted. As far as he was concerned, the conversation was over. The thought of that man taking his daughter out made him feel sick.

'I'm going to bring him to say hello,' she said resolutely. 'Then you'll see.'

A few days later she did just that.

Giorgos did not move from his position, grateful that he did not have to shake hands. It was a strange introduction.

'Baba, this is Takis,' Andriani called to her father.

'*Hairomai*,' Giorgos said, under his breath. 'Pleased to meet you.'

'*Kalispera*, Kyrie Kazaras, *kalispera*.'

It was an artificial situation given that Stakakis had been to the *periptero* before and both men were aware of it. Giorgos recoiled from his strong, musky scent. He must have used a whole bottle, he thought, to sweeten himself for his daughter.

Conversation was not going to continue.

'I'll see you later, Baba,' said Andriani, as brightly as she could.

Giorgos did not watch as they got in the car and drove off, but he heard the slam of doors and the pull of the engine as it sped away.

Sitting for all those hours alone, he had plenty of time to try to come to terms with what was happening to his daughter. He began by blaming himself for letting her read all those magazines and for all the big ideas that they had given her. But there she was, living with her old father and dreaming of a more glamorous life. What could he offer her? She had already been scornful of the potential fiancés he had suggested for her, sons of various local shopkeepers and even a couple of his late wife's distant relatives.

He could not stand the thought of Stakakis anywhere near his daughter but there was nothing he could do. At midnight, he locked up, returned home and went to bed. He lay awake all night, waiting for the sound of a key in the lock. At five in the morning, Andriani returned.

Early the following afternoon, Giorgos nodded

off on the padded chair inside his cramped cubicle. The heat, which had built up inside the kiosk like an inferno, combined with a sleepless night, had affected the usually resilient old man.

Several customers came and were puzzled by Giorgos' absence. In many decades, they could not recall him leaving his position inside his cabin even for a minute between the hours of six in the morning and twelve at night. Some of his customers were slightly irritated. Cigarettes were out of reach, so they would have to come back later, but for most other things they could leave a few coins on the little counter or even a note with an IOU.

An hour or more into his deep slumber, the sound of the coin spinning on the metal plate disturbed Giorgos. It was fifty cents. Concealed within the darkness of the kiosk, he remained invisible, but when he looked up he saw a hand reach in for some matches. He recognised the Rolex and shrank back slightly, keeping as still as he could. The man took some chewing gum and, to Giorgos' horror, a packet of condoms.

The old man waited until Stakakis had turned away before he got up. He watched him approach his car but just as he was about to get into it another vehicle screeched to a halt close by. A short, scruffily dressed man sprang out and stood between the furniture salesman and his Porsche. When Stakakis tried to grab the door handle, he slammed his hand against the door to prevent him from getting in.

All this happened within a few metres of the *periptero* and, on an afternoon when there was not even the rustling of leaves, Giorgos could hear every word.

'I need my money now. I've been waiting for nine months. What are you going to do about it?'

'You'll have to wait—'

'I've *been* waiting.'

Stakakis remained calm. His cool confidence, his cockiness, his smoothness were unchanged.

'Look, the bank has refused me a loan, and I've got no cash. I have the business. That's all. And customers aren't buying. You know what it's like out there.'

Giorgos assumed that Stakakis was telling the truth. He knew that the furniture shop had been offering 75 per cent discounts because his daughter had mentioned it and everyone knew that such sales were a sign of desperation.

In fact, Stakakis had sold only one thing in the past six months: a small glass side table that had been bought by a young couple. Not a single chair, nor stool, nor even one of the fancy tablecloths that were made to measure for the huge dining tables, had been shifted.

'Give me another fortnight,' he urged. 'I'll sort something out.'

Giorgos could see Takis Stakakis' back and watched the sweat spread across his blue shirt. The calm exterior was an act. The old man knew there must be big loans on his business. Everyone had them. Nobody drove round in a car that cost nearly one hundred thousand euros without borrowing money.

Then Giorgos saw the man collapse soundlessly to the ground. He disappeared from view and the old man realised he must almost be lying on his newspapers.

Less than a second later, the Porsche Cayenne

was gone.

The old man peered out of the little back door. He saw quantities of blood flowing into the gutter and the man slumped, lifeless, on the pavement. His magazines were ruined.

The street was still deserted in both directions. Giorgos took his stick and walked away as fast as he could. Within minutes he was inside the doorway of his apartment block and in another forty seconds the old lift had clanked its way up to his second floor flat. He let himself in quietly and sat on a chair in the dark hall. His main aim was not to disturb Andriani, who would be taking her siesta, but his heart was beating so furiously that he was afraid she might hear it.

He sat there considering the options that were open to him. If he turned Stakakis in, there was a chance that his only child would never forgive him. On the other hand, how could he harbour the secret of a man he hated more than anyone in the world?

A full thirty minutes passed before he quietly let himself out of the flat and walked back towards his kiosk. As he turned the corner to the main street, he could see that it was full of people and flashing lights. The area around the *periptero* was cordoned off.

In the days that followed, the police gathered information. Several of Giorgos' customers who had been in the area that afternoon confirmed that he had not been in the kiosk at the relevant time. The citizens of Panopoli were creatures of habit. They all passed by the kiosk at the same time each day and confirmed that Giorgos must have taken a break at the time of the murder. It had been the hottest day for a decade, so the *periptero* owner's explanation that he had, for the first time since anyone could remember, gone home for a nap was not queried. The streets around the kiosk had been similarly deserted so no one could have witnessed what took place.

* * *

Every single inhabitant of that small town came briefly under suspicion and all of them were questioned. The murdered man had been stabbed directly in the heart with a very standard blade, the kind that is found on a penknife, such as many men use in their business to split open packaging.

When the victim was eventually identified, the heat went out of the investigation. He was an immigrant from Albania and there were rumours that he had been involved in a drug ring.

A week went by.

'Baba,' said Andriani, one evening. 'You remember that red leather suite?'

Giorgos grunted.

'Well, *Ta*kis said he'd give it to us at cost price!' The way she purred her boyfriend's name made his stomach turn.

'*Agapi mou*. We don't *want* it here.'

Andriani stormed out, frustrated by her father's attitude.

Takis Stakakis came to the kiosk that afternoon. The old man, whose legs were not strong at the best of times, almost felt they would give way beneath him.

'*Kalispera*, Giorgos,' Stakakis said, with greater familiarity than before.

Giorgos said nothing.

'Why don't you come to the *kafenion* some time?' the younger man said. 'Drinks will be on me. I'm out of debt.'

Giorgos looked him in the eye. He hated loan sharks, and had a friend with a business in the town who had been terrorised by them. But he detested this smooth operator, this murderer, a thousand times more and wanted him out of his daughter's life.

'You know I never leave the kiosk,' he answered coolly.

Takis Stakakis lit one of his expensive cigarettes and inhaled deeply. Giorgos felt his penetrating stare but did not lose courage.

'And in fact you still owe me,' he added.

Stakakis continued to smoke, nonchalantly flicking ash onto the pavement. 'Really?'

'Yes. Five euros.' Giorgos watched Takis Stakakis' expression change. 'For the matches and a couple of other things you took last Friday. You only left fifty cents.'

Stakakis dropped his cigarette butt into the gutter and, in silence, fished a note out of his trouser pocket. He placed it carefully on the counter and, without meeting Giorgos' eye, got back in his car.

With immeasurable satisfaction, the *periptero* owner watched him drive slowly away. For the last time.

One Cretan Evening

The tourist invasion was over now. The shop that made its living through sales of pink lilos and cheap bikinis from Taiwan was now shut until spring, its windows firmly boarded up. Roadside tables now groaned beneath mountains of grapes, and olives steadily ripened, ready for harvesting in December. The passing of summer brought new fruits, welcome rain and, for local people, this was the loveliest of seasons. They were alone again and the clear, sweet air allowed them to breathe.

The real machinery of this Cretan village continued to run well beyond the departure of the foreigners. The *zacharoplasteion* still baked its daily quantities of sweet pastries and the best of the tavernas remained open even though the owners of the others had now gone to their winter homes. The priest conducted his services in the tiny chapel on the water's edge.

Life resumed its quiet, ordered ways. Widows in black dresses, their fabric as densely ebony as the day they had begun to mourn, sat on their doorsteps, away from the men, who entertained themselves with backgammon. Dice gently tick-tacked against the side of the board as the players whiled away the hours, moving counters from one triangular space to the next. Counters clicked together in conversation, more talkative than the men themselves.

Their knowledge of each other's lives went so far back into earliest memory that these septuagenarians had little to say to one another. They almost breathed in unison. They would discuss some piece of local news, perhaps the election of a new deputy mayor or a birth or death, but the wider events of the world at large, a crisis in the money markets or an earthquake in Peru, did not touch them even for a moment. Their universe was this small seaside village, this square, the same one where their fathers and grandfathers had sat before them.

Only the elderly lived here now. Most young people had long since deserted, escaping to the bright lights of the island's capital or Athens and only returning with the tourists for a week or two during August to remind themselves of where their ancestors had once lived.

Even now, with night falling, the men carried on playing and drinking their raki. There was a stillness in this moment. All day long, shadows of trees had danced against the pale faded walls and now the curtain had been drawn across their stage. Afternoon became night, as though a candle had been snuffed.

For the men outside the *kafenion* the transition of daytime into night went unnoticed. The tossing of dice, the refilling of small tumblers of the clear, syrupy fire water, the silent communication between them continued as before. Light or dark. It was all the same to them.

In spite of its almost noiseless arrival they were all immediately aware of the arrival of the taxi. For a moment their game of *tavli* ceased and they turned to stare as it passed. More lovingly cared for than a millionaire's limousine, the vehicle's polished chrome wing mirrors reflected the gleam of the dim street lamps.

It was not a number plate they recognised. All the drivers from the nearest big town were known to them, but this one was from further afield, from Heraklion.

When it drew up further down the street, they watched as the door of the passenger seat opened and a man got out. He was incongruously dressed, as though for a funeral or wedding, a slim figure in a dark suit, and they could just make out the neat shape of his hair. More than that, they could not see. He was a figure in silhouette.

After summer, the arrival of a stranger was relatively rare. In July and August, tourists came and went leaving behind them their money and, less desirably, their carelessly discarded rubbish. Now, only the very occasional outsider appeared, wanting to experience some of the island's legendary hospitality. By coming out of season they hoped to be welcomed in for raki, to be offered new olives and even invited to play backgammon.

The woman who owned the *kafenion*, Despina, came out to the front of the café and leaned against the doorway. She had heard the taxi and assumed it meant business. Clearly its passenger was not yet going to come her way. The old men shrugged and Despina retreated into the bar. Perhaps he would return later.

A thin stray of a dog had stirred as the man passed and now got up to follow him. The animal's emaciated condition made him little threat and after a hundred yards or so the man dropped the stone that he had picked up to scare away this wasted mongrel.

Walking purposefully down to the end of the street, his fingers pressed against the smooth, cool contours of a key.

One of the old men looked up from the backgammon board.

'Maria,' he said quietly to the others. 'Maria Makrakis.'

There was a muttering among them.

The man was aware of being observed and could feel the eyes of the village's residents upon him, but he did not turn. He needed to find something and only then would he return to speak to them. The two-roomed house was at the end of the street and the door, once painted deep blue, was now back to the bare wood with only the odd patch of its original colour.

His hand sweated a little as he grasped the key. Now he was turning it in the lock, marvelling at the way this door, even after ten years or more without use, still opened. The mechanism seemed miraculously to clunk and turn and soon he was pushing open the door to be enveloped by the smell of the past.

In the gloaming he struggled to see his way across the room and flicked a cigarette lighter to guide his way. The shadows of a room untouched by time leaped about him and his memories were stirred to life by the shapes of a table, chairs and even the icons on the walls, though curiously he had never been inside this house.

The truth was that nobody at all had been inside for the decade since its owner had passed away. There had been no one to tidy her things, to air the room upstairs or to fold away the sheets that still lay askew across the bed. Though devout, she had been despised and unloved, her spinster state making her an object of suspicion and derision. She had not grown up in the village and though she had lived there for nearly fifty years had always been regarded as a newcomer. This was how it had been in those days. No one could recall her having any visitors, or any friends; she was the outsider and the island's famous hospitality had not even once been extended to her. The place smelled of abandonment and dust.

The man had been watched entering the house but no one stirred. They did not feel protective towards it. Their concern was no greater than it had been for the woman who had lived there, who had existed in the shadow of rumours that she could never dispel.

The men were whispering among themselves and the women too, though the two groups still kept their distance.

'What's he in there for?' they asked each other. 'How did he get a key?'

By now the stranger had looked in the bedside cabinet and underneath the bed itself and was going through every drawer in a small chest in the corner of the downstairs room. They were all empty except for the last, which contained a small prayer book. Opening the cover, he held up the small flame to read the inscription:

'To Sofia Taraviras with love'

It was what he had been looking for.

He slipped the book into his pocket and emerged once again into the gloom of the street, carefully locking the door behind him.

Now he approached the *kafenion* and nodded his greeting. None of the men smiled. No one spoke. Despina was waiting for him. The man was much older than he had at first appeared. The dusky light had obscured the silver greyness of his hair and the deep lines on his face. He was no younger than the men who sat outside, but he was a city type, a businessman, obviously wealthy.

'What do you want?' she said. The brusqueness of the question surprised him.

'What do you want to drink?' she said, this time more politely.

'Coffee please, with sugar,' he answered, his accent revealing that he was from Athens, not from Crete.

'So what business did you have at Maria Makrakis' house?' she asked bluntly.

'Maria Makrakis?'

'Yes, the woman who lived in that house.'

'I don't know a Maria Makrakis,' he replied. 'My sister lived there. Her name was Sofia Taraviras.'

'Sofia Taraviras . . .' the woman repeated, puzzled. 'I don't think so.'

'Look,' he said firmly, producing the prayer book from his pocket. He carefully opened the cover and showed the inscription. 'Sofia Taraviras. I found it in the house. That was what I came for. It was my sister's.'

He handed it to Despina, who stared at the pale handwriting on the page.

'But the woman who lived in that house was called Maria Makrakis.'

'Well, she may have called herself by that name, but she was born Sofia Taraviras and this was given to her at her baptism.'

Despina closed the small leather-bound book, well worn with age and use, its pages as fragile as butterfly wings.

'Let's go and sit down,' suggested the

elderly man. 'It sounds as though there was a misunderstanding.'

Despina felt herself go pale. Maria Makrakis had lived in that house for longer than she could remember. In fact she had lived there before Despina was even born and her parents had always warned her against going too close. She had not questioned her parents. Children never did in those days.

'All I can tell you is this. Before I was even born, my older sister Sofia brought disgrace on the family and was despatched from Athens.'

The man paused to take a sip of his coffee.

'At the age of sixteen she had a child and my father sent her away. As far away as possible. To Crete.'

'But the woman in that house had always lived there. As long as anyone could remember. We were told she was a witch,' Despina said quietly. 'We were told not to go near her. And we never did. In fact I don't think I ever heard her voice.'

'Well she wasn't a witch,' said the stranger firmly. 'She was just a woman who had made a single mistake. She paid a high price for it, I think.'

Despina looked thoughtful. 'So why are you here now?'

'I only found out about her a few months ago when this came.' He produced the key from his pocket. 'It came from the priest. He was the only person who knew her story. She had told him everything, but being the priest he presumably never saw fit to share her secrets with the village. He had found the address of the family home. Look, it's written here.'

He turned the first page of the prayer book and

there, on the reverse of the inscription from Sofia's godfather, was an address. It was written rather proprietorially in neat schoolgirl script. An Athens address.

Despina listened in silence.

'There was some aunt of my father's who had lived here in this village and so this was where she was sent,' the man continued.

For her entire lifetime, Despina, like everyone else of her generation, had ostracised this woman without questioning why and now she felt the force of this community's shame. This 'Maria', this 'Sofia', had been forgiven by God, but never by His people. They had never even given her a chance.

Soon after, Sofia's brother left in the taxi. All he took was the precious prayer book. It was the only thing he had come for and he could feel its warmth in his pocket.

Early the next evening, as light faded, even the men who rarely stirred from the *kafenion* went to say prayers for the woman who had died alone. Whatever the old woman had done in her past, tonight it was they who needed absolution.

Autumn was a time of new beginnings here, not a time of melancholy endings, and the following day, Despina went in to Sofia's house. She threw open the shutters and the light flooded in.

The Butcher of Karapoli

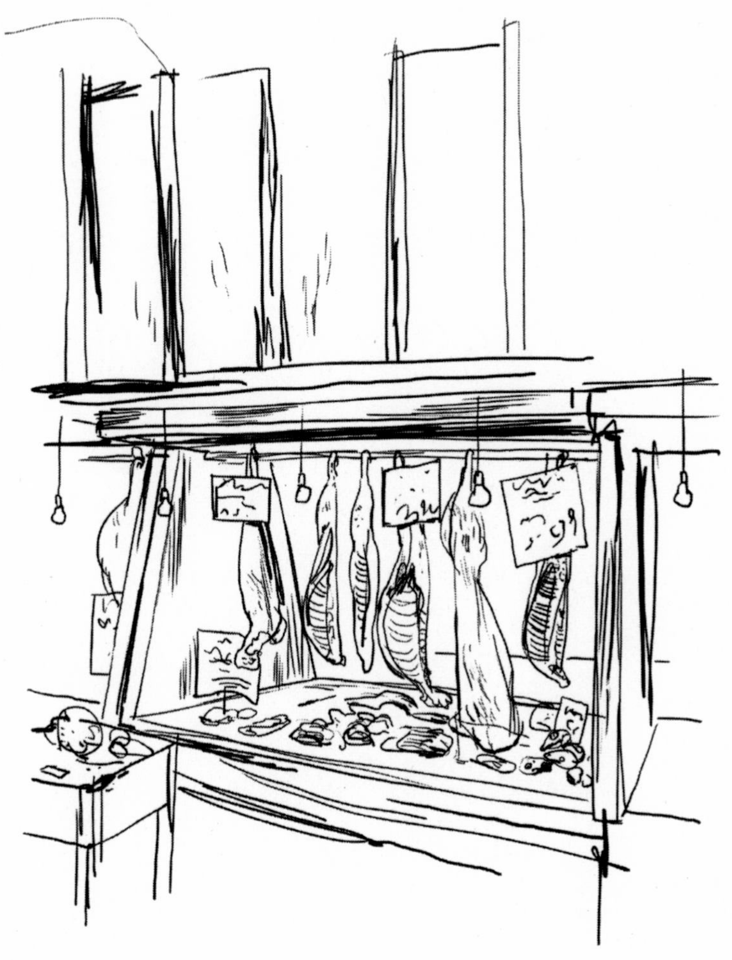

The market building in Karapoli had been built in the 1950s and was still the pride of the town. It was of metal construction, with a frosted glass roof, brick walls and a tiled floor, and was designed in the shape of a Greek orthodox cross, with four alleys, one for fruit and vegetables, one for meat and dairy, one for dry goods such as sugar and lentils, and the fourth for fish. At the centre was a flower stall.

In summer all the produce in the Manadaki market remained cool, and in the winter shoppers could wander at their leisure from stall to stall without fear of getting wet or cold. Everyone in the town had been delighted when it opened, particularly the mayor after whom it was named, and it was meant to mark the beginning of a new chapter in the history of a town which had been devastated by the occupation and the civil war that followed.

Stallholders had less space between them than they had once enjoyed in the street, so they jealously guarded every square centimetre that they rented from the municipality. Any crate that strayed into a neighbour's area was soon shunted back into place.

Shopping was a daily performance for every housewife and many of them would spend two hours inside the market—making it a social activity as well as a practical one. The ladies of Karapoli took the task seriously, prodding, poking, squeezing, sniffing and sampling before making their selections. Feta cheese, for example, might require half a dozen tastings—the bowls of cheese were identically white, but each had a subtly distinct flavour.

Meat was a different matter. There was no dithering or browsing. The only decision a customer ever made was made once: which of the three butchers to patronise. In this town, loyalty to a specific one was passed down through the generations and upheld with religious conviction. Everyone dogmatically maintained that *their* butcher's meat was from the best pastures in northern Greece, that it had been hung for the right amount of time, that the cuts were better, the value greater and the freshness superior. People rarely changed their views or habits in Karapoli.

The families who had been purveyors of meat in the town for as long as anyone could remember were Lagakis, Petropoulos and Diamantis. At the present time there was a father and a son in each business.

Even though she was not a resident of the town, Anna Dexidis knew which butcher she had to patronise. For longer than she could recall, she had been coming to stay in Karapoli every Easter and summer. Both her mother and her father were doctors in an overstretched hospital in Athens and could never spare more than a few days off, but each year happily left their only child in her grandparents' gloomy house, certain that the crisp air close to Ioannina would be better for her than the polluted atmosphere of the capital city.

Anna was adored by her grandmother but even being spoilt rotten for weeks on end did not help her homesickness. She felt cut off from her school friends back at home, and even though they had lived in the town for their whole lives her grandparents did not seem to know other couples with grandchildren, so for Anna they were lonely and isolated months. Her grandfather was always the stricter of the two and after an incident when, aged seven, she had accidentally broken a plate and been smacked, she was very wary of him. To her dismay, though her grandmother had recently passed away and her university days were almost at an end, Anna was still expected to make the long journey to Karapoli twice a year.

That year, she took over all the chores for her grandfather, attempting to do the housework as neatly as her *yia-yia* had done (and failing) as well as cooking (equally inadequately). Even as a younger man, the town's former postmaster had always been short tempered, but he had become more irritable and tyrannical with age. Anna now realised how much her poor grandmother had put up with, and was counting the days until she could return to Athens.

The only task Anna got right was the shopping, because old Alexandros Dexidis issued such strict instructions that she could not go wrong. Her aging *pappous* gave her no choice about where she should buy their food and precisely what she should get. When it came to meat, she was obliged to go to Diamantis. She had been a vegetarian since the age of fifteen, so she performed this duty with a certain disgust, knowing that she would push her own portion to the side of her plate.

'You must *never* go near that *malakas* Costas Lagakis or his son,' he would tell her firmly, cursing the man even to his granddaughter. Sometimes he would add another comment for good measure: 'The man's a devil,' he might say, darkly. 'I wouldn't put anything past him.'

Anna's grandfather maintained that Costas Lagakis had tossed some meat over the wall into their courtyard and poisoned their dog. The incident had taken place four years before but his anger seemed to grow with time.

'Five other people lost their dogs that month,' he would rant. 'And none of them were Lagakis' own customers. That's a fact.'

The mystery of the dead dogs had preoccupied the town for many months and never been satisfactorily resolved. Rumour had become fact as far as the old man was concerned. Costas Lagakis was a dog-murderer.

The story buzzed around inside Anna's head every time she went to the market where, in order to reach Diamantis, her prescribed butcher, she had to pass not only Lagakis but Petropoulos too. The latter flirted with every woman who went by and they all had to endure his standard repertoire: offers of a kilo of good sausage or some nice breast of this or that. He was vulgar just like his father before him, but Anna had become oblivious to the stream of innuendo that slipped off the butcher's tongue, like tripe into a bucket.

By contrast, neither Costas Lagakis nor his son Aris ever bothered her; in fact when they saw her coming they always turned away and busied themselves, carefully threading small cubes of lamb onto skewers or scrubbing one of the thick wooden blocks that stood in front of the meat cabinet. She felt the tension as she passed.

That day, her grandfather had ordered an extra large pork steak. It would be the last meat he would eat for some time, as Lent was to begin the following day. She knew he would be even more irascible with the change of diet, and it had puzzled her since childhood that a man who seemed so ungodly observed such a ritual.

Petropoulos was hoisting a whole pig onto a rack. There was a perfect incision the length of its body through which its guts had been removed. Hearts, lungs, liver, brains all now lay in separate tubs, divided up and on display, sold more cheaply than the flesh. Why was it that the organs that had once powered the animal were now almost valueless? It seemed the wrong way round. It was an endurance test to come to the butchers' alley. Anna was disgusted by everything to do with meat and even the smell of the place made her want to retch.

Now that she was older, she sometimes even came up with a retort to Petropoulos' banter. Today she was momentarily distracted by a huge pan of lambs' heads, jumbled together as if randomly massacred. Pairs of eyes stared out and a notice had been rammed into one of the skulls: *Kefalakia freska: 1 euro to ena*: Fresh little heads—1 euro each.

'That one's got his eye on you,' joked Petropoulos, pointing at one of the gruesome faces.

She tried to keep her own eyes firmly focused on the butcher at the end of the row.

A moment before a small lump of soft beef fat, the size of a single worry bead, had dropped from Petropoulos' counter. Camouflaged against the white of the tiles, it was invisible to her as she marched purposefully towards her goal and under her weight the substance spread immediately over the sole of her shoe.

Aris Lagakis always noticed how Dexidis' granddaughter passed his stall with her head in the air, as though he did not even exist. He knew that his father and the old man disliked each other intensely, but the girl's disdain was close to rudeness.

That day, he was busying himself at the front of the stall arranging some liver and labelling it, but he was conscious of her every step. She was more than a metre away from him but he caught her scent, a sweet contrast with the sour smell of raw meat.

Perhaps Aris realised even before Anna did that her feet were sliding from under her. In an immeasurably small fraction of a second, he detected the change in her gait. His reactions were fast. The calf liver that he held in his hand fell with a dull splat to the ground as he darted forward, catching her just before her head would have hit the ground. Anna was no weight, but to help break her fall he landed with her on the tiles and found himself cradling her in his arms.

In reality, everything happened fast, but for Anna it was as if in slow motion. She felt herself flying through the air, lifted, horizontal and for a moment suspended. Then she found herself lying on the ground, her only reaction one of mortifying embarrassment. She noticed the lump of offal that Aris had dropped close by and began to struggle to her feet. Only then did she realise that there was a man behind her, holding her by the shoulders and helping her up.

Her fury and humiliation took over. She could feel the stares of customers and stallholders alike.

'It wouldn't be so *dangerous*,' she said furiously, 'if you bothered to clean up properly!'

Aris had never made eye contact with this young woman as she had been sure to avoid it, but now they stood face to face he saw that her eyes were translucent blue and cold with anger.

When she looked down she noticed that her arms were smeared with blood and there were spots of red on her dress too. Had she grazed herself in the fall? Noting the absence of pain, she realised that the blood was not her own.

'Look!' she said. 'My dress is *ruined*!'

Aris opened his mouth to speak, wounded by a sense of injustice. If he had not saved her, she would undoubtedly have been injured. In an attempt to make her understand, he held up his palms to show her that they were smeared with calf's blood too and this was what had marked her dress. But she had already stormed off. Lagakis' son was the last person in the world she would have wished to fall in front of.

'When you go to the market, I don't want you going anywhere near that stall,' her grandfather had so often repeated. 'Nowhere near it. Do you understand?'

The young butcher picked up the liver and mopped the floor. He was meticulous about his immediate area and knew beyond doubt that his neighbour, Petropoulos, had been responsible for the slippery patch which had caused the fall. He saw that Anna was now making her purchase from Diamantis and would soon be making her way back towards him. She could not avoid it. He could see that she still simmered with anger and turned away as she approached.

The 'crossroads' at the centre of the market, past which all customers had to go, was occupied by a single florist, Maria Sophoulis. That day she was making up bunches of roses, shrouding them in bright plastic netting and adding a garish bow. She stood back to admire her artistry. It was Savina's name day, and she had been doing brisk business.

From her vantage point in this prized central position, Kyria Sophoulis could see all four alleys and knew everything that went on in the market. The florist was the all-seeing eye. Customers' flower-buying habits gave her plenty of information: who was friends with whom, who was making up or breaking up, who was having a flirtation or an affair. Nothing escaped her attention.

'Are you OK?' she asked Anna. 'That could have been a bad fall.'

'I'm fine, thanks,' Anna said, reddening, wanting her moment of humiliation to be forgotten.

'Thank goodness that young man caught you.'

'*Caught* me? *Did* he? I thought he just picked me up.'

'I saw it,' the florist confirmed. 'It was as if you were flying. He threw himself under you in the nick of time. You would've been concussed if he hadn't been there.'

'But—'

'There really isn't a *but*,' said the florist firmly. 'He saved you and you should be grateful.'

'Well he shouldn't leave slimy bits of meat on the floor in the first place,' Anna retorted.

'He doesn't,' said Maria. 'Everyone knows it's Petropoulos who is the dirty butcher. It's not just his tongue.' She read Anna's quizzical look. 'Petropoulos is always getting fined by the municipality for not cleaning his area properly—you're not the first one who has slipped there. Kyria Eleftheria fell and broke her wrist a few years ago. Exactly the same place you did.

Lard. That's what it was. Lard. But you can't blame the lard. You blame the person who dropped the lard. Aris is a good lad. Clean and tidy.'

Anna remained silent. Nothing could change her opinion of the Lagakis family. She had grown up to think of them as the enemy and her grandfather had dripped too many dark comments into her mind for them to be so easily erased. The death of the dog had been only one accusation.

The florist saw herself as a peace-maker and even more often a match-maker. Flowers were never just flowers; there was always a meaning in them. Unlike meat.

'I think you should go and say thank you,' she continued. 'If you were a man, I'd make you buy some flowers. But that's no good for a woman, is it? I think a smile and a nice thank you will do the trick.'

'It's his father,' mumbled Anna.

'What has it got to do with his father?' Maria asked. 'His father isn't even here today.'

'My grandfather said something about him, that's all. About the dogs.'

The florist was firm but dismissive.

'You shouldn't believe everything you are told,' she said. 'There are just as many people who think it was one of the mayor's men. There were some strange things going on round about the time of the last elections. But no one ever proved anything.' The florist picked up a length of ribbon and snipped it in half, muttering under her breath, '*Panagia mou*, this town. Nothing ever changes.'

'What do you mean?' asked Anna with innocence.

'You obviously don't know what's behind all

the rumour-mongering that goes on in this place, do you?'

Anna shook her head. 'No, I don't really. I just know that my grandfather is still angry about his dog.'

'There are reasons why one person goes to this butcher and another goes to that one, and why they favour one baker over another,' she answered. 'Everyone in this town has alliances and grudges and there's a basis for all of them.'

'Tell me, then,' Anna urged.

'It goes back to the civil war. It poisoned this town,' Maria said. 'People are still bitter. Those who took against each other then are still against each other now—and some of them even pass it down to their children . . . and grandchildren.'

Anna looked down at the floor.

'Look, sit down for a moment,' the florist fussed. 'You do look a little pale after your fall.'

She sent out for some coffees and carried on making up her orders.

'So why does my grandfather hate Lagakis so much, if he had nothing to do with the dog dying?'

'They were on opposite sides. *Telos pandon*,' she said with finality. 'That's all there is to it.'

There had to be something more and Anna knew it. 'But his hatred seems to be *about* something. It's so extreme.'

Maria Sophoulis continued trimming her stems.

'I'd really appreciate it if you told me, Kyria Sophoulis,' urged Anna. 'I know my grandfather won't.'

'I just don't think I should be the one to tell you . . .'

'Nobody else is going to.' Tears of frustration

were beginning to prick Anna's eyes.

'You might not really want to know this.'

'Please.'

'Very well then. Shortly before the civil war came to an end, the bodies of six young communists were found in a barn just outside town. They were only kids, really. Two of them weren't even fifteen.' She stopped speaking for a moment. 'Lagakis was friends with them all, and the same age as the youngest. He was meant to meet them that night, but he was late. He claimed to have seen them being murdered. He accused your grandfather. Your grandfather supported the Right—but I assume you know that.'

Anna clapped her hand to her mouth and her eyes widened as Maria continued.

'There was no trial. Some people on the Right had been killed just before and accusations and counter-accusations were flying. But the suspicion never went away. You'll still find people round here who think your grandfather was responsible.' Maria swallowed hard and looked at the young woman. 'He was known as the Butcher of Karapoli.'

Anna thought she was going to be physically sick. She did not want to believe such things of her grandfather, but she could not dismiss the feeling that they could be true. She stood up, afraid her legs might not carry her, and walked away, uncertain how she would face the old man.

When she returned home, he was sitting in his usual chair, reading his newspaper. She could not look at him. Claiming a migraine, she put the lump of meat still wrapped in its waxed paper into the fridge and went to her room.

All night she tossed and turned. *The Butcher of*

Karapoli. The words haunted her.

The following day, with some trepidation she tried to lead her grandfather into conversation about the 1940s, but she could see his anger rising. She realised she would never have the courage to confront him.

That evening she picked up a copy of his newspaper and read it through, appreciating for the first time how far to the right Alexandros Dexidis really was. The editorials were overtly fascist and she had to admit to herself that her silver-haired *pappous* was not at all the kindly old man that grandfathers were meant to be. If he *was* 'the Butcher', it would make sense of his lack of friends and her own father's reluctance to stay for very long in the town. She knew little about the civil war except that such atrocities had been perpetrated and she could not dismiss the idea that her grandfather had been involved one way or another. It was a small town, after all. Perhaps she would never know for sure.

When she went into the market the next day, the meat alley was almost deserted and Aris was polishing the glass front of one of his chiller cabinets. Until Lent was over, business would be slow.

She walked straight up to him. 'I just wanted to say thank you,' she said. 'And sorry I misunderstood.'

'Don't worry,' he answered. 'It's OK.'

Aris Lagakis knew about the animosity between her grandfather and his family and he surmised that she must know too. It seemed absurd that the events of fifty years ago should still cast a shadow over his own generation. However vicious the war had been, the vendettas were not theirs.

‘Shall we go for coffee some time?’ he asked hopefully.

‘Yes,’ she answered without hesitation. ‘I’d like that.’

Anna felt light-headed. Perhaps she was a little concussed after all.

The Lesson

It was early September but the temperature was still close to forty degrees. Two children were on their way to the schoolhouse for the first time.

Giannis' mother was aware of her son's palm sweating in hers. Fotini's mother could feel her daughter's fingers clamped tightly round her own. Neither woman knew who was more anxious, her child or herself.

The population of the village had diminished in recent years. Many younger people had gone away to work abroad and only came back in the summer months, when the cafés on the main street would once again be full. 'It's just like the olden days,' the elderly ones would then murmur with watery eyes. In August, they would celebrate the feast of Agios Titos, the local patron saint, and the circular open space at the edge of the village would be filled with trestle tables and plastic chairs. Within a week, the village would be half empty once again, the chairs roped together and stacked against the wall of the church. A few of them might be used again at Easter when the lamb was roasted and a reduced number of villagers gathered to celebrate.

Nowadays older children were bussed to and from the nearby town for their schooling, but there were still twenty or so *paidia* in the village between the ages of six and eleven, enough to fill the primary school, the *demotiko*.

Many of the adults in the village found themselves taking their offspring to the same building they had gone to as children. Many of them had even been taught by Kyria Kakanidis, who had arrived thirty years before.

It would be fair to say that she prepared the children well for the stage that followed, known as the *gymnasio*. In some ways she was the reason why some of the youth in the village left and never returned. At their next schools they found themselves at the top of the class, winning scholarships and even places at universities abroad.

'If you till the soil properly, then the seeds will germin-ate,' she said to the parents. She drew the analogy from early memories of watching her father working in his *kipos*. It might only have been a single *stremmata* of land, but the way he sieved every last grain of its earth until it flowed like sand through his hands was the reason for its fecundity.

'It's all in the preparation,' he said to his daughter a thousand times.

* * *

Kyrios Kakanidis had always put great emphasis on creating neat, orderly rows, which he made using small wooden stakes and lines of string against which every seed was planted and every seedling transferred.

'Organise the plot, maximise the output,' he said to his daughter, and such mantras ingrained themselves into her own thinking.

Kyrios Kakanidis certainly achieved great results. While neighbours struggled to grow a few tomatoes and beans out of the same stony and infertile soil, he had gluts of every kind of vegetable that grew above the ground and below. Each day, from May to November, he would load up a table on the main street with whatever he had harvested that day, and place a rusty tin at the front for the money. Onions, carrots, courgettes or peppers—there was always something perfectly ripe and ready for picking.

As a child Katia would watch her father shake out the contents of the tin into a wooden box, which would then disappear. For her entire childhood she remained slightly mystified by what happened to the money, since her parents seemed continually short of it, but when the day came for her to go to college in Larissa, she knew what they had saved for during all those years. The carefully hidden drachmas were enough for her teaching qualification.

For most young people, education was a passport out of the village. For Katia Kakanidis, it was her return ticket. Her ambition had never been anything other than to work at the school where she had received her own early education. She wanted to implement her own ideas on how children should be taught, and doing this in the very place where she felt so many mistakes had been made in her own childhood gave a pleasing sense of completing a cycle, rather like her father using the seeds from one of his tomatoes to cultivate the following year's crop.

When Giannis and Fotini arrived at school, their mothers greeted each other. Only two years apart, the women had both spent the early years of their education in this place.

'*Kalimera*, Maria.'

'*Kalimera*, Margarita. How is little Fotini today?'

Her mother answered for her. 'A bit anxious.'

'The same with Giannis, I think.'

The small boy scowled, he did not want to be

seen as cowardly, though inwardly he trembled. He had not been out of his mother's sight much before and he knew that the moment was coming. There were only twenty children but it seemed an enormous crowd. And it was not only the number of them, it was the size of them—the older ones looked huge.

Little Fotini had more confidence. She had an older brother who had already left the school and she was unafraid of the bigger children milling around outside the door.

'I'll see you in just a few hours,' her mother said to her, letting her go.

The child held out her hand to Giannis.

When Katia Kakanidis saw the pair of them for the first time, that was how they were. Hand in hand.

She came towards them and leaned down. '*Kalimera, paidia*. Good morning, children.'

Both the children looked up at the bony-faced woman. They saw big shadows round beady, black eyes, and a pointed chin. Wisps of dark hair floated around her head and the rest was swept into a bun. As she leaned in close, Giannis noticed a tiny spider climbing towards her scalp.

He was mesmerised.

'You must be Giannis,' she said. 'And you are Fotini?'

Fotini nodded.

'Well?' the teacher asked, looking at Giannis.

Giannis was still mesmerised by the spider who had by now disappeared into the forest of wispy hair. Fotini squeezed his hand tightly. He nodded vigorously without speaking.

'You sit there,' Kyria Kakanidis said, indicating

an empty seat at the front to Fotini. 'And Giannis, you sit behind.'

There was another boy already sitting at Giannis' table. In front of him was an open book with large pictures and he sat with his head in his hands, staring at the words. He did not look up when his new neighbour sat down, nor did he shift across to give him space at the table they were meant to share.

When she had been appointed as schoolmistress in the 1980s, Katia Kakanidis had made some innovations. In fact, they were not steps that modernised the school, but the reinstatement of some of the old traditional ways. Her predecessor had, among other things, replaced the old wooden desks with formica-topped tables and arranged them in a semi-circle round the teacher's desk. Kyria Kakanidis did not approve of the fact that the tables had to accommodate two pupils and lamented the disappearance of the single wooden desks. All she could do was to drag the tables back into strict rows.

One of the features of the old desks had been their individual inkwells, but she put a large bottle of ink on her own desk at the front of the classroom and insisted that the older children revert to the use of fountain pens.

'You can't write properly with a ballpoint,' she said briskly when they complained. 'Our beautiful Greek characters were created in ancient times. They didn't have biros then, so you are not to use them now.'

Another of her retrospective actions was to put up posters of the alphabet, mathematical equations, and quotes from philosophers. She did not believe in having children's work on the walls.

There seemed no point in displaying anything less than the ideal. Why make a virtue of imperfection? Everything should make them aspire to improve whatever the struggle, and in her own judgement the pupils' progress validated her methods.

Giannis and Fotini got into the habit of walking to school together holding hands. Sometimes they would come into the classroom and sit down at the same desk.

'Up!' Kyria Kakanidis would call briskly as she entered the room. 'Up! Up! *Up!* You well know where your desk is, Giannis. So *sit* there!'

There was no logic in their separation. No one was allowed to speak in the classroom unless they were spoken to or unless they were asked to read something out, so what was the harm in being next to someone you liked?

Fotini loathed her neighbour, the priggish Elpida, who curled her hand around whatever she was writing in order to hide it. Every child of her age was learning their letters and it was incomprehensible to Fotini that the other girl felt a need to possess the alphabet. It did not after all 'belong' to anyone.

'What's so secret?' she whispered loudly, breaking the code of silence. From her older brother, she had learned to be bold. Elpida ignored her.

Giannis meanwhile was bruised by the vicious pinches from the boy with whom he shared a desk. 'Shared' was not really the appropriate word. The fat boy, Panos, took up more than two thirds of the space, often shoving Giannis so hard that he would find either himself or his books on the floor. Kyria Kakanidis was always ready to chastise Giannis, suspecting him of deliberately drawing attention to himself. Much worse than anything, Panos smelled. On hot days the odour was almost asphyxiating.

The school comprised two spaces: the room where the children learned their lessons and the yard where they played. They were supposed to run about in the winter to have some exercise, but the girls would form small groups and huddle together for playground gossip. Boys would kick a ball around in the dust.

Throughout the first term, Giannis and Fotini kept apart from the others at playtime, talking earnestly or sometimes playing a game they had made up with small stones. Kyria Kakanidis observed them, irritated that they did not keep to the groups that she tried to establish. The sight of their heads bent together in conversation offended her.

'Nits!' she would cry out, when she saw the strands of their dark hair almost blend together. 'Nits! That's what happens if you sit like that!'

In the second and third years of school, Giannis and the increasingly obese Panos were made to stay at the front of the class and the studious Fotini was put at the back. Most days, Giannis was to be found perched on the edge of Fotini's desk, chatting with her, several minutes after lessons should have begun. Kyria Kakanidis, always alert to their disobedience, would sneak up on them and slam a ruler down onto the desktop with an ear-popping *thwack*.

'Back to your desk, Papalambos!'

In the early years of her career, the ruler would have landed on flesh, stinging the back of a thigh or hand, leaving its red mark for an hour or so. She was a little nostalgic for those days. Punishments had been well defined, like the mark that lingered on a child's leg just long enough to be remembered but not so severe that it had not vanished before the bell rang for end of school.

In their final year, Kyria Kakanidis felt that she had failed to make Giannis and Fotini behave as other children. Obedience seemed to her a basic prerequisite for moving on to the next stage of life.

'Giannis,' she said icily to the boy, who had shot up in height in the past year and now almost met her eye to eye. 'If you are incapable of doing what you are told, I will have to find another way of reminding you. Into the corner! Face to the wall! Hands on your head! Until I tell you!'

For many hours, he remained in the same spot, unmoving in the heat. The other children went out to play, drank thirstily from the fountain in the yard, ate their snacks and came back to the schoolroom to resume lessons. Meanwhile, Giannis stood.

He was in front of one of Kyria Kakanidis' posters. It was an anatomical drawing. Every bone of the human body, each muscle and sinew, was identified. For four hours, Giannis stared at it, reprimanded by the teacher from time to time if she saw him shifting or fidgeting.

An ache began to set in at the base of his back, then gradually crept down towards his feet. His arms throbbed with pain until he could feel them no more and eventually one of them fell from his head and dangled limply by his side. It was numb. Then his left arm did the same.

'Papalambos! Hands on head! Now!'

As the feeling returned and the fierce tingling that went with it, he managed to raise them once again. His eyes smarted with pain and humiliation but he was determined not to lose control and cry. Another hour passed and his legs almost buckled under him as he felt his right foot lose feeling. He kicked the wall in front of him in an attempt to restore it.

'Keep still, Papalambos! If I see you do that again, you can stand there again tomorrow.'

The end of the school day came and the children dispersed. Fotini sat quietly at her desk. She knew Giannis would not move from his position until he was dismissed by their teacher and she wanted to wait for him as usual.

Her presence angered the teacher. If it were not for Fotini, then Giannis would not have needed to be reprimanded in this way.

'You can go now,' she said, addressing the pair of them snappily. 'If you both followed the rules, I wouldn't have to remind you of them.'

Even when given leave, Giannis found himself momentarily unable to move. It seemed to take an age before feeling returned to his limbs. Fotini then took his hand and silently led him out of the classroom.

There were many more occasions when Kyria Kakanidis felt compelled to punish her pupil. Giannis spent several hours of every week standing in the corner.

When the day came for Giannis and Fotini to move on to their next school, there was no sorrow in their farewell and the schoolmistress was glad to see the back of this pair who had never respected her 'rule of rows'.

* * *

The years passed. Giannis and Fotini got married the year they left university and were among those who found opportunities that would keep them away from their village, rarely visiting, even in August. Fotini became a lawyer and Giannis trained to be a doctor, eventually specialising in rheumatology.

Giannis loved his work even though the hours were long and the working conditions were almost intolerable. As in every corner of Greece, government cuts meant that most hospitals had reached crisis point and the overburdened doctors were regularly ill themselves either from stress or from sheer exhaustion.

One Friday afternoon in July he was doing an extra shift for a colleague on sick leave. With his own list, Giannis would have scanned the names of patients at the beginning of the session, but all the people he saw that day would be strangers to him, so there seemed little purpose. His last appointment was with a woman.

When she came in, leaning heavily on a stick, she was so bent over that her face was obscured, but as soon as she sat down he recognised the bright, beady eyes. Though her black hair had turned to grey, the expression on her face was unchanged.

On Kyria Kakanidis' side, there was not a flicker of recognition. Two decades had completely changed Giannis. A small nose had become a much bigger one, freckles had vanished and his once straight, silky hair had gone curly over time. As far as she was concerned, he was a specialist who would cure her of the crippling pains that now kept her awake all through the night. Her belief in the medical profession was absolute.

He swallowed hard, trying not to betray anything in his voice. 'So, Kyria . . .'

'Kakanidis,' she said, to help him out.

'Tell me,' he said briskly. 'What can I do to help you?'

'Well . . .' she said. 'I think I might have the beginnings of arthritis.'

'What are your symptoms exactly?'

'When I wake up in the morning,' she said, 'I feel so stiff it's almost impossible to get out of my bed. And when I do, I can't straighten up.'

'And are you in pain?'

'Constant,' she answered. 'Terrible.'

'Well, we need to see whether this is progressive, so it will be necessary to take measurements over a period of time in order to monitor whether your stoop is worsening. If you could get up for me, please . . .'

Katia Kakanidis rose with difficulty from her seat and stood next to the scale fixed to the wall.

'If you could just excuse me for a moment . . .' said Giannis, rising from his seat. 'There is something I need. Just stay there please.' And with that, he left the room.

For a few minutes he leaned against the wall outside, his heart racing. Even her voice evoked bitter memories and recollections of pain.

The heat in the building was stifling. The air-conditioning had broken down many days before and the atmosphere was rancid with disinfectant and sweat. Giannis walked out of the main entrance, crossed the car park and stopped on a piece of dry scrubland carpeted with cigarette butts. He leaned against a tree and lit up. He never smoked at home because Fotini hated it, but at work he regularly succumbed. It was the only way he managed to relieve the intense stress of working in this dilapidated, neglected hospital. There were usually several other members of staff doing the same.

For the first time in his career, he realised he would be unable to treat a patient. He could not look after someone unless he cared.

He smoked first one cigarette, then another, and the time slipped by. When he looked at his watch, he realised that more than thirty minutes had passed. Kyria Kakanidis had been the last patient on his list, so he felt no need to hurry as he strolled back towards the building.

With the deference she reserved for people in the medical profession, Katia Kakanidis had remained standing by the wall for the entire time Giannis was out of the room. She had not dared sit down.

It had only been a few minutes before the pain took hold, but she stubbornly remained standing. Every bone in her body cried out to sit, but if the doctor found her on a chair when he returned, it would seem as though she was not following orders. She resolutely resisted the temptation.

By the time Giannis reappeared, the elderly woman was fighting back her tears.

'So sorry to keep you waiting,' he said briskly. 'Let's just measure you before you sit down.'

He took a note of her height and then asked her to lie on the couch, where he examined her spine. There was clear evidence of disintegration. Sometimes even he marvelled at the level of pain people endured before eventually coming to a doctor.

'So,' he said, finally. 'Take a seat.'

She sank down into the chair opposite Giannis' desk and watched as he made a few notes.

'Is there anything you can give me, Dr Balinakis?'

Giannis looked up. 'I'm not Dr Balinakis,' he said. 'He is away this week.'

'Oh,' she replied, with an unmistakable hint of desperation. 'But my question is the same. Is there anything you can give me?'

'Not at the moment,' he said. 'Come again in a month's time. Dr Balinakis should be back by then.' He got up, to make it clear to the patient that the appointment had come to an end.

'Thank you, doctor,' said Katia Kakanidis, struggling to her feet. She then paused for a moment. A name inked inside the white coat, carelessly thrown onto a hook, caught her eye. With difficulty she turned the handle with both her clawed hands.

As the old woman hobbled out, Giannis stared at her retreating back and realised that he could make out a knobbly ladder of vertebrae through her thin blouse. The door closed behind her. With a jolt, something occurred to him. In all likelihood, the old lady was probably the reason for his being there. Those long ago hours of studying the human frame might have been the catalyst. Shame stabbed him like a scalpel's blade.

Out in the corridor, the old woman was still waiting by the lift. He quickened his pace.

'Kyria Kakanidis . . .'

She lifted her head and Giannis caught her beady stare.

'I'm sorry,' he offered.

'So am I, Dr Papalambos,' she said, with a catch in her voice. 'So am I.'

The Pine Tree

Snow fell, deeply, crisply and evenly. Slowly the row of pine trees turned from green to white and their needles sparkled. A crimson-breasted robin puffed out his chest. It was the perfect white Christmas.

Santa Claus looked out from between the trees. His huge, round belly was accentuated by a wide belt and his head moved from side to side, as he mimed his maniacal 'ho-ho-ho'. Over his shoulder was slung a sack from which spilled out a dozen presents wrapped in metallic red and green.

And beneath one of the trees nestled a crib. Mary and Joseph bowed over the manger, while shepherds and wise men queued patiently to catch a glimpse of the baby. The bearded figure in red velvet who stood behind them was as tall as the trees and all five of the sheep by the crib would have fitted into the palm of one of his big gnarled hands. Everything was out of scale.

In the centre of this tableau, there was a woman, tall and slim-waisted, with bare, strong arms. Claire caught sight of herself as the figures in the seasonal fantasy faded and the polished shop window mirrored her reflection. She looked into a pair of blue eyes.

She had been transfixed by these symbols of Christmas, conceived in northern Europe, manufactured in China and now in a window display in a hot and dusty street in Cyprus. They seemed so incongruous here. This was a city where pavements still shimmered in November and where snow was never more than a fantasy. People strolled down the promenade every day of the year, contemplated a swim in the sea and sought shade under the palms.

And yet here was an entire shop given over to selling tinsel and tat, an emporium of seasonal symbols for customers who yearned for the kind of cold snap that Claire herself was happy to have left behind. The sight of them did, however, provoke a strong twinge of homesickness and a wave of longing for the fog and ice of northern England and her family's annual get-together.

She was nervous about the prospect of her first Christmas away from home, but she would not be alone. It was more than the lure of sun and the certainty of daily blue skies that had brought her here. It was Andreas. Like so many English women before her, she had taken a one-way journey for the sake of a dark-eyed foreigner.

Though they had met in Manchester, where Andreas was studying, he had no plans to be away from his *patrida* for long and if she wanted to be with him there had been no question of compromise. Soon she followed him to the sunny island where he had been born and his intense love gave her no cause to doubt her decision.

Andreas returned to his village near the capital, Nicosia, and Claire found herself an apartment on the edge of the city. The view was predominantly of the other white-washed blocks that surrounded her in all directions, some of them only a few decades old but their paintwork already chipped and the plaster falling away in lumps from the concrete walls. What the architects had failed to visualise in their blueprints of these fast-expanding cities were the air conditioning units hanging off at angles, the jumble of solar panels and satellite dishes, and the metal rods that protruded from the roof tops like walking sticks. Lines of garish laundry pegged out on every balcony completed the picture of chaos.

There was no lack of opportunity in Cyprus for an articulate expatriate willing to work hard for little pay and Claire now had a job in a bookshop and a routine that was not so unlike the life she had left behind. There were details that differed, however. The working day was longer and the heat made it seem longer still as she struggled home on foot, carrier bags bursting with quantities of seasonal vegetables and household goods whose names she still struggled to decipher. Though corners of this island were almost English, it was nevertheless distinctly a foreign country. In her apartment, with the doors and windows thrown wide in an attempt to catch the breeze, the air was filled with the competing sounds of a dozen different TV stations. Some evenings, driven demented by the relentless cacophony of blaring music and voices, she would shut the windows and, though the heat was stifling, at least she could then enjoy the silence.

It was not the ex-pat life that her friends envisaged, of late nights and parties and daily visits to the beach, but she was strangely contented. She and Andreas saw each other at weekends and for now that had to suffice.

* * *

That December day, she was standing outside the Christmas shop waiting for Andreas to pick her up. He was finally to take her for the much-anticipated visit to her prospective in-laws. In-law, to be precise. And she was nervous. Such an introduction carried more significance here than it would in

Yorkshire.

'I know she'll like you,' said Andreas attempting to reassure her. 'But don't be put off if she seems a bit unfriendly.'

'Why should she be?' asked Claire, with faux naivety, knowing already the reputation of Greek mothers.

'It's just the language barrier,' he answered. 'She won't really be able to talk to you, that's all.'

As they drove up into the hills above Nicosia, they could see the faraway spaces of the part of the island occupied by Turkey. The division of the country was rarely mentioned by Andreas but, with the clear view of a Turkish flag provocatively carved into the hillside, Claire was reminded of this uneasy separation. Soon they reached his village and the streets narrowed. The buildings were warmly characterful and most of them had been home to many generations of the same family. Several of them seemed to be held up by thick boughs of bougainvillea and vine that were now inseparably entwined.

'Look,' he said, as they passed a blue door. 'There it is.'

An elderly woman, slim, with birdlike features, appeared at the entrance of one of the larger houses. She looked frail enough to be blown over in a breeze. Her arms were folded and her face expressionless. Until she caught a glimpse of her son. And then it was as though the sun had emerged from a rain cloud.

Andreas parked his car in a dusty space at the top of the hill and they strolled back down towards his home. His mother waited on the doorstep, her smiling eyes now fixed on her son. Although she was as thin as a stick, Kyria Markides had the strength to embrace her son with bone-crushing warmth and effusive cries of '*Angele mou!* My angel! *Matia mou!* My eyes!' and all the while she looked over his shoulder at Claire and fixed her with a steely glare. In spite of the warmth of the day the young woman almost felt her heart freeze.

They went inside the house and gradually her eyes became accustomed to the gloom. They sat awkwardly at the table for some time as the elderly creature in widow's weeds bustled about in the kitchen. Claire looked around her. The walls were covered in the same icons that she had seen in other Cypriot houses, but in addition there were perhaps thirty photographs. Some of them were wedding pictures but most of them were formal portraits of the same man, handsome, moustachioed, proudly wearing army uniform.

'Your father?' enquired Claire.

'Yes,' Andreas replied.

'You look quite a lot like him . . .'

'That's what my mother always says. Sadly, I don't remember him.'

Claire had known that Andreas had no siblings. She also now saw how much this only child was doted on and adored by his mother. She suddenly felt the awkwardness of being here. It was not just the nostalgia for home, a place where even if it did not snow on Christmas Day, the likelihood of frost was strong. It was also the sense of being an outsider, particularly here, in this house.

She sat quietly through the meal. A few other relatives had joined them: cousins and their children, three aunts and two very aged uncles. Claire smiled when she was spoken to, though she did not have a clue what was being said, and took a little from every plate that was handed to her, even eating one of the minute baby birds, *ambelopoulia*, cruelly caught and killed on their maiden flight. She did not want to let Andreas down, but at the end of the meal, when glasses of fiery *zivania* had been swallowed and it was time to depart, she was exhausted from keeping up the pretence of enjoying herself. Kyria Markides gave her a cursory handshake as they left.

The atmosphere in the car on the way down the hillside was tense. Claire felt that she had done her best but the iciness from Andreas' mother had been worse than she had anticipated.

'Why does she have to be like that? What is wrong with these Greek mothers? Why are they so possessive?' The tension had been building in her since the moment they'd arrived and she could not contain her anger.

Andreas did not answer and Claire was unable to make out his expression on this dark moonless night.

A few minutes later she repeated her question.

'Well? Why?'

His silence only provided further provocation.

'Your mother will never accept me,' she said with resignation. 'I'm an outsider here and I'll never be anything else.'

They were now driving into Nicosia. Claire glanced out of the window and noticed they were passing the same shop window she had seen this morning with its fake pine trees and falling snow.

She also realised that he had now taken a turning that led away from her area of Nicosia but after a while he drew up.

'There's somewhere I want to take you,' said

Andreas.

They walked, apart, down a street illuminated with festive decorations and in the far distance Claire could make out a Christmas tree. It was standing in the middle of the pavement, not illuminated with fairy lights but festooned with ribbons. As they got closer she saw that there was something stranger still. Instead of baubles, this tree was hung with photographs, black and white pictures, mostly of men, with words and a date underneath. 1974.

'Look,' said Andreas. The caption under the picture he was holding read: 'Giorgos Markides'.

The photograph was faded and had evidently been there for many years.

'But why is his picture here?'

'My father was one of the "disappeared",' explained Andreas. 'Like fifteen hundred others, who vanished when Cyprus was invaded by Turkey, he has not been seen since. The pictures keep the memory of them alive.'

Andreas had only just been born at the time and his mother had waited, and waited, expecting each day her husband's return. Every day she had lit a candle in the church and prayed, meanwhile lavishing on her son all the love she had for Giorgos and much more.

Claire touched Andreas' arm, half-expecting him to draw away.

'I'm so sorry,' she said. 'No wonder she fears losing you. It makes perfect sense.'

Andreas looked at her and smiled.

'I think it will take a while for her to realise that you're not going to take me away from here, that's all,' he said.

They stood on the pavement contemplating this strange tree that was there not just for December but for every day of the year, and Claire's urge to be in England left her entirely. This was where she wanted to be, far from frost and ice, with sweet balmy air around her and the sight of this pine without snow.

The Last Dance

Somewhere in every neighbourhood in Athens, whether smart, tatty or totally run-down, there is a window full of fairy tales: a photographer's studio. The romantic wedding tableaux they create will be on show in a couple's living room for the rest of their days. Unless they divorce, of course.

There was one such studio up the street from Theodoris' apartment and over the years he had walked past it a thousand times. He had long since ceased to notice it, until today. Recently several shops to either side had closed down but it seemed that people still had money for lavish wedding photos, if not for ceramics or antiquarian books.

In his diary, he had an appointment with his fiancée and her mother to visit a similar place so, for the first time, he paused to see what might be in store for him. He perused the window, observing that the backdrops tended to reflect the bride's choice of gown. If she had gone for something fluffy, then they would select a more fanciful backdrop, a ruined Venetian castle perhaps; if she had opted for a more formal style, then perhaps a classical landmark, even the Acropolis, would appear in the background. Pretty much everything could be faked, even the glow of a bride's perfect skin or a groom's pearly white teeth.

Every bride in the fairy story was a beauty and every groom a prince, and around the happy couple there always shone a halo of light. It was as if they were, in the moment of their nuptials, somehow transcendent, blessed by both God and gods.

The man generally wore a standard, well-cut suit,

often a white one if it was a summer wedding, but the focus of every image was the bride. Her gown eclipsed all else.

Theodoris had accepted early on in his engagement that he would be peripheral to the wedding plans, almost to the wedding itself, now only a month away. It was his second engagement and he already knew what to expect.

* * *

A decade before, he and his ex-fiancée, Agapi, had lost all the battles with her parents. They had never got as far as a visit to a photographer.

They had first met in a bar close to Syntagma, where there was live music every night. The volume had precluded conversation and before they even spoke, they found themselves dancing together. The words of the song were romantic, and by the time it came to an end Theodoris felt he had already declared his love for the beautiful girl he held in his arms. Only then did they introduce themselves. It was a lightning strike, a *coup de foudre*, *keravnovolos erotas*, the most powerful feeling either had ever experienced. Both assumed that this love would be their last.

Although it was ten years earlier, he remembered the final conversation with Agapi almost word for word. Whenever he thought of it, the searing pain of their separation returned.

'If they're making our lives hell now,' she had said, her eyes full of tears, 'it will be no better when we are a married couple. I have watched it happen with my sister.'

Theodoris was only twenty at the time and had

no defence. For many months he observed with growing discomfort the way in which Agapi's brother-in-law was treated by her bullying parents, and he realised that the tide of their disapproval of him combined with a desire for dominance over their daughters was all-consuming. Like her sister before her, Agapi had the promise of a spacious, three-bedroomed flat, built on the floor above the parents' home. The apartment would be a wedding gift, a dowry, and Theodoris could not bring anything of equal significance to the marriage. This offering of bricks and mortar, concrete and glass, in Kolonaki, the most fashionable area of Athens, was the bedrock of their future.

Even without being told to his face, Theodoris knew instinctively what his prospective in-laws had disliked about him. His main crime was to come from a small island and to have an accent that gave it away. His father made a reasonable living from fishing, but in the eyes of Agapi's mother he must be a peasant, and an uneducated one at that, since there were no schools on the island.

Theodoris could not fight such views and knew they would never change. Gripped by sadness, he had taken back the ring with its speck of solitaire diamond and he and Agapi had separated. He was too young, too weak, for such a fight and it had been a dream-shattering outcome for a boy who believed that love was what mattered.

In the following decade, he put the thought of marriage to one side and focused on his studies, in the process becoming an increasingly eligible husband for any potential mother-in-law. Once the results of his final law exams had been confirmed, he found himself with the time and inclination to accept an invitation to dinner from the senior partner of the firm where he worked.

It was immediately clear why he had been invited. The blushes of their daughter gave away their game. He followed the inevitable flow of the next few months, feeling himself being eyed up like a piece of ripening fruit by the parents. This time, it was in someone else's interest to bring him into a family through marriage. There were no sons to take over the father's business and Theodoris knew he would 'do'.

Nefeli had pale skin and dark wavy hair. There was nothing particularly remarkable about her looks but she was sweet enough and adored Theodoris from the first meeting. A man who worked for fourteen hours a day needed someone to worship him for the other ten. The engagement lasted for a year, the time it took to plan a sizable wedding celebration. Nefeli's mother chose the dress for her daughter, the flowers, the church, the date, and the photographer.

Now, as he stood looking in one photographer's dust-streaked window, his phone rang. It was his fiancée calling to confirm their appointment with a more upmarket equivalent in central Athens.

'I hope our photographs will be more natural than the ones I'm looking at,' he said, trying to sound light-hearted. 'Mmm . . . yes. *Endaksi*. OK. That's good. See you later.'

* * *

A month after that, Theodoris found himself at the church, accompanied by his *koumbaros*, his best man. It was at one of the largest churches in Athens, a popular place for society weddings, and in the summer months there was, at times, something close to nuptial gridlock, as one ceremony swiftly followed another. Theodoris had arrived as the last of the guests from the previous wedding were leaving and he surveyed them warily, unsure whether they were coming or going. The only way he could tell was if they were already clasping a tulle-wrapped package of sugar-coated almonds, a gift to wedding guests as they left the church.

He and his *koumbaros* carefully stepped over a length of flex as they entered. An elderly man was vacuuming up a carpet of rice which had been tossed over the bride and groom. It was hard to speak over the noise, but he hovered near the door to greet his first guests, many of them strangers to him, and half an hour or so passed as the church refilled and he waited for his bride. Theodoris' father and two elderly aunts arrived quite late, dressed in black, anxious and ill at ease. His father looked proud but out of place in this unfamiliar city.

At the appropriate moment, Nefeli appeared. She had chosen a romantic, fairy-tale gown and looked more beautiful than he had ever seen her. He handed her a bouquet of flowers and the ceremony passed without a hitch. The priest had spent the break between ceremonies lubricating his voice with raki and honey, and as a result he glided effortlessly from note to note in the chanted responses.

When they all spilled from the church, a new crowd was already gathering outside. The two groups mingled, women from the different parties jealously eyeing up each other's expensive wedding outfits: bright tailored suits in raw silk with matching shoes, dress and jacket ensembles with contrasted piping, flimsy frocks that were more suitable for a nightclub than for a church, and, concealed beneath coats, tell-tale flashes of silver and sequins. Age and size were disregarded here. Every woman wore something fitted tight and close to her body. They had all taken as many hours to get ready as the bride.

A huge fleet of cars wove its way through the streets of Athens to a sprawling international hotel south of the city. It was a place that catered for conferences in winter and weddings in summer and left nothing to chance with either clientele.

The hotel could host four wedding receptions on any one day, as long as they were slightly staggered. All the guests arrived through the grand entrance before being siphoned off to one of the four wings, named appropriately after the winds: *Boreas*, *Notus*, *Eurus* and *Zephyrus*. North, South, East and West. The only facilities they shared were the cloakrooms and the space outside the main entrance, where anyone, whether guest, staff, or driver, could gather to smoke.

Theodoris and Nefeli's guests flowed through the entrance into the allocated ballroom, where six hundred places were laid for a five-course meal. At one end of the room, they stood to have a cocktail before taking their places at huge circular tables. Beyond the dining area there was a dance floor, where guests would eventually enjoy dancing to a live band—traditional Greek music as well as more modern pop. Even the timing of that would be managed, to the last second, by the hotel.

Forty-five minutes from the arrival of the first guest, they were all seated and there was a loud drum roll. Beneath the stage, Theodoris and Nefeli waited on a small platform, ready for a hydraulic mechanism to raise them up. As they appeared, there was a ripple of applause. The guests had been waiting with growing impatience for the grand entrance and were more than ready to eat. They were hungry. After all, many of them had been lured here by the promise of a little social networking, but they also expected a good dinner.

Following the starter, which left the guests hungrier than before, six waiters came to every table, each bearing two plates with silver domes. At a hidden sign from one of them, twelve silver domes were lifted with split-second precision to reveal the main course beneath. It was a flamboyant gesture, but what was revealed did not quite match up to the anticipation: a piece of lamb the size of a biscuit on top of which was perched a small pile of twigs that, according to the printed menu, were shredded potatoes. A swirl of dark sauce had been daintily painted onto the plate in the shape of two initials: N and T.

Theodoris glanced across the table at his father who was looking down at his plate. It was the first time the old man had ever left his home on Miltos and he looked totally out of place in this vast ballroom. Everything must seem strange and alien to him, and Theodoris could read his father's mind as he looked down at the plate in front of him. If he had married an island girl, a whole sheep would have turned on a spit, musicians would have been playing and wine would have flowed from a barrel. The food would not have looked like a work of art, and by now everyone would be high on *tsikoudia* and atmosphere. He caught his father's eye and tried to raise a smile. His aunts sat one on each side of their brother, like bodyguards in black. Self-conscious about their accents, they did not speak to the other guests, but occasionally muttered comments between themselves.

As the dome-lifting ceremony was performed, there was a momentary lull in the general chatter. It was during this brief, silent hiatus that Theodoris heard the strains of familiar music from the next door room. It was quickly drowned out again by the clatter of cutlery and resumed conversation, but Theodoris needed to get some air. He felt as though he had been punched in the stomach.

He touched his bride on the arm and told her he would be back in a moment. Leaving his meal untouched, he left the room.

Through the partitioning, on either side of the *Zephyrus* suite, two other wedding receptions were in progress. The bride and groom were yet to arrive in *Boreas*, but in *Notus*, they were well ahead. They had long since had the ceremony of the lifted domes, and delicate sculptures of frosted fruit balanced on a thin slice of chocolate torte had been eaten and cleared away. A few minutes before, the bride and groom had performed their first dance and it was the final verse of their song that Theodoris had heard.

*   *   *

As the door closed behind him, Theodoris saw a woman in white beneath the vast crystal chandelier.

A few other wedding guests milled about round the edge, but in the middle of the great circle of red carpet she was alone. After so many years, it was as if his heart, rather than his eyes, recognised her. Agapi.

'Theodoris,' she said, as he made his way towards her.

'My God, Agapi! It *is* you . . . Have you just . . .?'

'Yes, just.'

'Congratulations,' he managed to say. 'You look beautiful.'

There was an awkward silence.

'I thought I just heard our song . . . Did you play it?'

'Yes . . . for the first dance. It's still my favourite,' she said, quietly. 'Music isn't really Nikos' thing, so he let me choose whatever I wanted. There seemed no harm in it.'

They stood close, smiling into each other's eyes, drowning in the pleasure of seeing each other again. For a few brief minutes, they were oblivious to where they were and their reasons for being in these anonymous surroundings that could have been anywhere in the world.

The double doors to the *Zephyrus* ballroom had swung open.

'There it is again,' Agapi said, trying to smile. 'Seems like it's everyone's favourite tune.'

Without thinking, Theodoris put his arm around Agapi's waist and began to twirl her around, both of them caught in the moment, light-headed with the strange pain of seeing each other again after all these years. Theodoris was only aware of Agapi's sweet, familiar voice singing the words close to his ear.

'S'agapo yiati eisai oraia
S'agapo yiati eisai oraia
S'agapo yiati eisai esi.'

'I love you 'cause you're beautiful,
I love you 'cause you're beautiful,
I love you 'cause you're you.'

The band continued to play the tune, over and over again, as they rotated beneath the chandelier.

Moments later, Theodoris' best man appeared and desperately tried to attract his attention. Theodoris continued to turn, and each time his *koumbaros* reached out to tap him on the shoulder his friend melted away and out of reach.

'Theodoris!' he called finally, in some desperation. '*Theodoris!*' He could see that the groom's eyes were closed. So finally he had to raise his voice: 'THEODORIS!'

Now he had his attention.

'It's the first dance, Theodoris. Nefeli ... your mother-in-law . . . everyone . . . they're all waiting.'

The couple stepped away from one another.

'You, too?' said Agapi, looking at him quizzically. 'Today?'

'Yes,' he replied, feeling his voice almost fade to nothing. 'Today.'

They stood apart now. Agapi looked over Theodoris' shoulder and saw that her groom was approaching.

'You had better go,' she murmured almost inaudibly. 'You're late.'

Too late, he thought. I'm too late.

They gave each other one final glance and with a leaden heart Theodoris turned away.

Ideas and Inspiration

by Victoria Hislop

The stories in *The Last Dance* are not set in the familiar touristic landscapes of Greece. Most of these tales take place in more mundane places, in the towns and cities that are often bypassed by visitors and are less 'picture postcard' than the islands and beaches of the Mediterranean. For my first twenty-five years of travelling to Greece (my first trip there was in 1976), I was a tourist and I probably only saw the aspects of the country that the Greek Tourist Organisation wanted me to admire: ancient monuments, museums full of rare antiquities, golden beaches and picturesque tavernas with their clusters of painted chairs and tables.

In the past five years, since my novels were published there, I have been lucky enough to make many Greek friends and my experience of the country has changed radically. Many of them told me that I had been seeing their country through rose-tinted lenses and, although I could see nothing wrong in doing this, I invited them to show me things about their country that they considered more authentic and perhaps more gritty.

As a result, I have recently travelled extensively around Greece, visiting towns and villages which are either agricultural or semi-industrial and where there are no guidebooks on sale. Perhaps to the bemusement of my new friends, I have even found the less glamorous corners of Greece interesting and inspirational—though I have created fictional settings for these stories, sometimes combining characteristics of several different locations.

Inspiration for Sofia's house in 'One Cretan Evening'

As well as going to places that are not on the tourist map, I have also travelled out of the tourist season. The winter mood of a Greek city is the opposite of the carefree summertime atmosphere of its islands. Most visitors go to Greece when the heat keeps people outside on their doorsteps, sitting in tavernas and on the beach, so there is an image of intense socialising, leisure and, to be honest, very little work. All this changes in late

October/early November. From then until March, the climate is much damper and harsher and snow often falls. These are the months when Greece feels like a different country. The Greece of the *Mamma Mia* image is only one 'face' of this fascinating place, and I find its antithesis perhaps even more inspiring.

I have tried to write about some of the darker tones I have found in Greece, even while maintaining my positive views of the country and its people. Many of the stories in this collection take place in day-to-day, almost domestic, settings: the kiosk, the pastry shop, the market-place and the *kafenion*, which is a focus for the Greek male, just as the English pub is for the British.

A local *kafenion*

As well as the *kafenion*, another of the great Greek 'institutions' is the kiosk, the *periptero*. These have become part of the landscape since the first one was set up one hundred years ago, and there is one in almost every street. The *periptero* is a small, claustrophobic cubicle open almost all hours of every day, only shutting for a few hours at the dead of night. It sells all the essentials of life—newspapers, water, cigarettes, confectionary, soft drinks and so on. It is even more vital to Greek life than a corner shop in the UK. It intrigued me that anyone working inside a kiosk potentially saw more of what was going on in the street than anyone else, and might become an unseen witness to almost any crime. This was my inspiration for 'The *Periptero*'.

In 'The Butcher of Karapoli', I wanted to write about two things. The first of these was the way in which many Greeks seem to have enduring grudges or feuds. They do not easily forget a slight and I have sometimes seen this passed down through more than one generation (there is an element of this same trait in 'One Cretan Evening' too). Added to this, there are sometimes long-held memories of what took place during the Greek Civil War (1944–49). This was a bitter conflict, where whole villages were divided between Left and Right and memories of killings and reprisals are still vivid today. In the decades following the civil war, anyone who had fought for the communists continued to be persecuted in some way; many were exiled on islands or imprisoned on the mainland, and even when released they were restricted in the professions they could enter. The repercussions of this civil war continue even sixty or seventy years on. I wanted to show how it is possible for such bitterness to be passed on to subsequent generations.

In the title story, 'The Last Dance', I have written

about the tight hold that Greek parents have on their children. The styles of upbringing in Greece and the UK could not be more contrasting and Greek friends are sometimes as shocked by the British approach as I have been shocked by the Greek. The Greeks prefer to keep their children close, while the British tend to push them out of the nest so that they learn to fly. It seems to me that the Greeks often prefer to clip their children's wings rather than give them the freedom to go their own way, and one mechanism for ensuring this is to provide their daughter with an apartment close by (often in the same building). This 'dowry' then means that she will remain near, along with the son-in-law and then, at some further date, the grandchildren. The advantage of this is that parents will have someone to look after them when they get old and frail, and for the daughters it often means there is a ready-made babysitting/nanny service. At other times, however, this almost claustrophobic proximity of family members can create difficulties all of its own.

For the male protagonist in this story, and indeed for the girl with whom he has his 'last dance', the interference of the girl's parents will have an enduring, possibly catastrophic effect, on both their lives.

A year or so ago, my Greek teacher set me the task of writing a story with 'revenge' (*ekdikisi*) as the subject matter. Even though we think of it as a common theme of Ancient Greek tragedy, revenge is still very much a force in Greece today, so I naturally set my homework in the present. The slow-burning, unforgotten resentment of a boy for the treatment he received from a cruel teacher gave me a chance to write about the old-fashioned schools that I have seen in a few Greek villages, where pupils of every age are seated in one room. The school mistress herself is not so far from a teacher I once had, even though the pupil in the story is not me. Whenever I read or see a Greek tragedy, it seems to me that revenge gives a lifetime of suffering to the perpetrators themselves. Everyone loses out in Greek tragedy, so I thought I would try to twist this around.

I now know my Greek friends were right. I was seeing their country through rose-tinted glasses. But even with clear ones, I still find it endlessly fascinating and perhaps even more inspiring than before. I have now seen many more moods in Greece than I did as a tourist. The commonplace details which I think people cease to notice when they see them on a daily basis are the things I often find the most interesting, charming, different and worth writing about.

Fresh bread in a *zacharoplasteion*

It is impossible to be in Greece now and not to see and feel how life has changed for people in the cities. More shops and businesses close each week and restaurants are by no means as full as they were a few years ago. Many people are struggling to live on drastically cut wages, or are unemployed, and there is a palpable sense of anxiety, particularly in the larger cities. I have touched on the difficulties that Greece is facing in some of these stories, but have not made it a focus, because I think the nature of the country and its people remain the same. Even if fancy clothes shops are struggling, the traditional places like the *zacharoplasteion* and the *kafenion* continue to thrive.

A gift from a *zacharoplasteion*

These are the cornerstones of Greek life. I am always amazed at the style of extravagant gateaux and sweet things that continue to be hugely popular in Greece, and that are used to celebrate birthdays and saints days, with no expense spared. Food and the sharing of food remain a priority and I suspect will continue to be so, even when people are forced to use their own furniture as fuel to heat their homes (alas, such things are already being talked of in Greece).

A protest march in Athens

One very grey day last winter, a friend took me to see the chaos of a Greek tax office in central Athens. It was an extraordinary experience but out of the confusion and disorder, a story has begun to emerge. It would be naive to go into a bleak building of this kind in the middle of the capital city and not notice some of the worst aspects of bureaucracy, mountains of dusty files, antiquated computer systems, people apparently filing fingernails rather than paperwork. For me, this will become another 'Greek scene', another 'point of difference'. But that's for the next book. I hope readers might come back for more.

Victoria Hislop
March 2013